Ghostly Play

Lorna Shadow cozy ghost mystery - book 8

K.E. O'Connor Books

Chapter 1

I didn't know why I was tiptoeing. I was in my own home for goodness sake. This was the place I should feel most at ease, able to kick off my shoes and relax. Instead, I was creeping around barefoot, trying to find the elusive ghostly Amelia and figure out what she was playing at.

It seemed she didn't want to come out to play today, though.

Flipper was by my side, his nose pressed against my thigh as we continued skulking around the house. We went through the lounge, into the kitchen, and past the dining table.

I stopped our slow circuit by the back door and stared out at the first flush of spring dusting the trees with green.

"Why are you hiding from me, Amelia?" I whispered.

There was nothing but silence.

It had been like this since I'd returned to the house two weeks ago. Zach was convinced the ghost of his late wife was haunting him. Every time I tried to contact her, I got nothing. She didn't want to communicate with me.

This was surprising. Ghosts usually loved to bother me. Even when I didn't want them by my side, they were often there, pestering for my help and trying to get me to fix their problems.

I'd given up avoiding them and had accepted my fate as a fixer of ghostly issues. After all, if I was in their position and discovered someone alive could see me, I'd pester the heck out of them until they helped me to figure out my problems.

Amelia was different. She was staying silent, and that bothered me.

Flipper nudged my leg with his nose and looked up at me.

"You're not picking up on anything strange?" Flipper was excellent at detecting signs of ghosts. In public, he went under the guise of my assistance dog. In reality, he was the best friend you could ever want. Well, the best non-human friend. He was loyal and faithful and a perfect furry hot water bottle on a cold night.

Flipper looked out the glass door and barked. Jessie was out there, rooting about under a bush, her black nose buried deep in a pile of crisp leaves.

There'd be no chance of getting help from Flipper now. Whenever Jessie was around, they were always together, causing mischief and having a whole heap of doggie fun.

I unlocked the back door and let him out. "Go and play. And, just so you know, you're a rubbish ghost hunter."

He looked at me over his shoulder. He knew I didn't mean it. I loved Flipper to the moon and back and had done so ever since I'd discovered him abandoned as a puppy. We saved each other that day.

Gunner Booth strode into the kitchen, two empty mugs in his hands. He was off duty from his high-up position in the police. He wore faded black jeans and a checked shirt over a white T-shirt. "Morning, Lorna. How's it going?"

"It's going slowly." I closed the door. "How about you?"

"Oh, you know. The usual." He switched on the kettle. "I'm making more tea for Helen and me."

I smiled. Gunner and Helen. Finally, they'd stopped sidling around each other and were officially a couple. It didn't mean that they argued any less, but I had a feeling the making up was a lot more fun.

"I'm trying to persuade Helen to stay longer, but she insists you can't be late for your new jobs. It's all she's talked about this last week," he said.

I nodded. "She's always good at keeping people on track."

"That's what I like about her." Gunner grinned. "I also enjoy trying to get her to go off plan. When she lets her hair down, she's a lot of fun."

"And when she doesn't go off plan as you call it?" I cocked an eyebrow at Gunner.

His grin widened. "Then she's equally as great."

It was official. Gunner had it bad for Helen. So he should. She was my best friend for a lot of good reasons. She was funny, loyal, ditzy smart, and an amazing cook. She always had my back. I loved her like a sister.

"Have you seen Zach?" I asked.

Gunner fiddled with a teaspoon. "He had to get supplies for his new job. He said he'd be back by now."

I was worried. Ever since the revelation that Zach had been married, things hadn't been the same between us. It was my fault. As hard as I tried, I couldn't shake my frustration at him having hidden such a big thing from me. He probably would never have told me about Amelia if it weren't for the fact she'd started haunting the house. I hated secrets, and that had been a huge one.

We'd talked about it, a lot. Zach was genuinely sorry. I understood he'd made a mistake. He was such a typical guy, trying to solve things and not asking for help. Now we were both in this mess, and I couldn't see any way out. Especially if Amelia refused to communicate with me.

"Is there any sign of Amelia?" Gunner glanced at me.

"She's staying clear of me," I said.

"You definitely think she's here?" Gunner had been surprisingly easy to convince that I could see ghosts. Easier than Zach. Although I sometimes wondered if Gunner was just humoring me for an easy life.

"I'm not for sure, but Zach's convinced she's here. Have you had any things go missing?"

"Only my cookies," Gunner said. "I'm blaming Helen for that."

I had to smile. Helen was a demon when it came to anything sweet. Well, she loved all food. I was always amazed how she kept her curvy figure, eating the way she did.

"She'll make it up to you by baking more brownies," I said.

"I hope she does," Gunner said. "I'll miss her... cooking when you leave."

"She'll miss you too." The Booth brothers were hopeless at sharing their feelings.

"I said no to the tea." Helen hurried into the kitchen, a suitcase in one hand. Her blonde hair was tied in a neat ponytail, and she wore fitted green pants and a floral-patterned blouse. "If I drink any more, we'll have to make too many stops. We can't afford to be late."

Helen was particularly excited about this new position. Normally, she took on the role of seamstress or laundress. This time, she was putting a new set of skills to the test. She'd been hired to do the cooking. She couldn't be more thrilled. There was nothing Helen liked more than rustling up a new dish of treats. Helen was a feeder. I was delighted about that. I was a disaster in the kitchen. If it weren't for Helen, I'd have been surviving on instant soup and tuna eaten out of the tin.

"Baby, surely you can stay for one more drink." Gunner wrapped an arm around Helen's waist and pulled her close.

"There's no point in trying to sweet talk me." Helen made a half-hearted attempt to get away from Gunner, before submitting to his kisses.

I looked away, not wanting to interrupt their romantic moment. I couldn't help but feel a pang of envy. Ever since Zach's revelation about Amelia, I'd put up a barrier between us. He'd even spent a few nights sleeping on the couch after we'd argued. I hated the fact things weren't going well between us.

It wasn't so long ago that I'd thought a marriage proposal from Zach wasn't far off. But now, I couldn't be sure we even had a future together.

I looked around the kitchen. If only Amelia would show herself. We could figure out why she was here and get her out of our lives. Until she was gone, I couldn't see us moving forward. The ghost-shaped wedge between us was too big of a deal for me.

"No! We have to go. The Hudson's won't be impressed if we don't turn up when we said we would." Helen finally succeeded in getting out of Gunner's arms. She straightened her blouse and shot me an exasperated look. The twinkle in her eye suggested she wasn't all that upset over Gunner's interest.

"Isn't there anything I can do to convince you to stay?" Gunner asked.

"Not a thing. Are you ready, Lorna?" Helen asked me.

"I'm all packed. I was hoping to say goodbye to Zach before we left, though."

"Is he still not back?" Helen's smile faded. "He must have got stuck in traffic. He wouldn't want to miss you."

"I guess so." I wasn't convinced by that argument. Maybe he didn't want to say goodbye. But Zach had been going on lots of errands lately, and finding reasons to get out of the house. Maybe he no longer thought of this as his home and wasn't happy here. Maybe he wasn't happy with me.

I shook myself out of my glum thoughts. I had a new job to go to and had to concentrate on that. I ran up the stairs, grabbed my suitcase, and headed for the front door.

Gunner let Jessie and Flipper into the house. They bounded over to Helen and me.

"You can't both come with me." I petted them on the head. "Jessie, Zach will miss you if you don't stay here."

Jessie wagged her tail, ever hopeful she'd get to hang out with her best friend a bit longer.

"Say your goodbyes. It's time to go," I said to them.

Flipper nuzzled Jessie. She rubbed her face against his before turning and sniffing his butt. She was ever the lady.

I headed outside to give Helen and Gunner a moment alone. I was hopeful of seeing Zach's Land Rover puttering along the road. My heart sank. There was still no sign of him. Only Helen's small red car sat in the driveway, prepared for our journey down south and into the beautiful Kent countryside.

I loaded our cases into the trunk, trying not to listen to the smooching and sweet talk between Helen and Gunner as he walked her to the car.

The morning air was chilly, spring was still fighting with winter to break through. There were early blossoms on the trees and hints of green peeking up between the rich brown earth. It wouldn't be long before the winter sweaters went away and the frosts vanished from the grass.

"Come on. We can't be late." Helen hurried past me and hopped into the driver's seat.

I shook my head. Like I'd been the one dragging my heels and smooching with my guy. If only I had the chance to do that.

I let Flipper into the back of the car. He loved this car. It was his favorite place to take a long nap.

Climbing in next to Helen, I keyed in the GPS directions to our new home, the village of Old Tubbington.

We got to the end of the road, and Helen indicated a left turn. I looked both ways. I wasn't watching out for traffic, but for Zach. I really didn't want to leave without saying goodbye. It felt strange leaving without seeing him.

"I'm so excited about this job," Helen said. "I can't believe they took me on when I have no formal cooking qualifications."

"The family sounds relaxed." I settled into my seat and pushed away my disappointment. He wasn't coming home. "I did a bit of digging on them after Josie sent the information." Josie was my contact at Prestige Recruitment Agency. She was great at finding me new personal assistant jobs.

"They sound like new money," Helen said.

"They're internet millionaires. It's the son we'll be working for, Alex Hudson. Although, his mom hired us."

"I bet he's thrilled about that," Helen said. "His mom made him hire staff. I hope he's not some over-entitled brat who's difficult to work for."

"He is young," I said. "I've seen pictures of him online. In fact, he's everywhere online. This guy knows his way around the internet."

"He made his money in online apps, isn't that right?"

"Apparently so. He created a dating app that's popular," I said, "and loads of video games. He's on YouTube as well. He's got over a million people following him."

"What sort of videos does he upload?"

"Gaming videos. He's into fantasy violence games. Wizards and warlocks killing each other, alien attack stuff, and something called Bog Globs."

"How dreadful," Helen said.

"It's not my sort of thing either," I said. "I used to enjoy Pacman when I was a kid, though."

"Maybe he'll let us play some of the retro games if he even knows what they are."

"Perhaps he'll introduce us to a whole new world of online gaming fun."

"It'll not be like our old place then," Helen said, "all that good food by the seaside and lots of lovely wine."

"Not to mention two killers and a secret love child." I grinned at Helen. "I loved Cornwall, though. But with Honey selling the house and Julianne hiring a manager to look after the vineyard, there was nothing for us to do. We had a good six months down there. They did say we could go back any time we want a free wine tasting holiday."

"It's for the best we didn't stay any longer," Helen said. "And that job meant we could afford to furnish our whole house and have some money left over."

"Are you saving for something special?"

She tapped her fingers on the steering wheel. "Gunner has mentioned he might like a holiday."

"You're going away together?"

"Don't sound so surprised," Helen said. "We are dating."

"I had noticed. All the kissing and sweet talk is impossible to avoid."

Helen grinned. "You and Zach can come with us."

"It's not a terrible idea." I plucked at a loose thread on my sleeve.

She gave me a worried look. "Are you still having problems with the whole Amelia thing?"

"A bit. I still don't know what she wants."

"She's doing it deliberately," Helen said. "She wants to cause trouble because she's jealous of your relationship with her husband."

"They'd been separated for years before she died," I said. "Amelia has no claim on Zach."

"She might feel territorial, though," Helen said. "You're serious with each other, and Amelia doesn't like it."

"Why turn up now? She'd been dead for months before the problems started."

"It could be that she only realized Zach was serious about you when you moved in together," Helen said.

"I guess so. I just wish she'd either leave us alone or tell me what she wants. Then I can help her get it and get her out of our lives."

"Has any more of your stuff gone missing?"

"Amelia has stopped stealing my underwear, which is a good thing. But Zach is still having things go missing. It turns up in the oddest places. He found his razor inside his toolbox the other day."

"Amelia hasn't touched my things anymore," Helen said. "If she does, I'll have stern words with her."

"Good luck with that," I said. "She's ignoring everyone but Zach."

"You'll figure it out. You and Zach are meant to be together. No moldy old ghost will spoil that."

I didn't feel too convinced. "I hope you're right."

"I know I'm right," Helen said. "Now, sit back and relax. All you need to worry about is enjoying the scenery as we make our way to Kent and our lovely new jobs."

I forced myself to relax as Helen whizzed onto the motorway. She was right. I'd figure out the problems with Amelia and Zach.

I wouldn't let any ghost spoil our relationship.

Chapter 2

It was late in the afternoon when we arrived at the house in the charmingly named village of Old Tubbington.

From the cute little thatched cottages and beamed houses we'd swept past in the car, I'd assumed we'd be working in something similar. But the house in front of us was a large, white detached modern structure, made of chrome, concrete, and huge sheets of glass. The roofs were all flat.

"This is what they call a contemporary style dwelling." From Helen's wrinkled nose, I could tell she wasn't impressed.

"It's modernist." I climbed out of the car and let Flipper out. "Maybe it's an eco-home. Look at all the solar panels on the roof. The electricity bills are probably only five pounds a month."

"Give me a low-ceilinged cottage that leaks heat any day," Helen said. "Much cozier and full of character."

I looked up as I heard a small plane flying low over the house. It circled overhead before returning the way it had come.

The front door of the house opened. A woman with a dark neat bob, wearing a tailored cream suit, walked out. She strode down the steps toward us, her hand already extended. "You must be Lorna and Helen."

I smiled and shook her hand. "I'm Lorna Shadow. This is Helen Holiday." I looked around for Flipper, who was investigating a flower bed. "That's Flipper, my assistance dog."

"Good to meet you all. I'm Camilla Hudson. I spoke with your agency about you. I'm so glad you could come. We're in dire need of your services. Well, my son is."

"We're happy to help," I said. "I'm looking forward to meeting Alex."

"Excellent. My son's a genius, but he hasn't got an ounce of common sense. I assure you, if I didn't keep a sharp eye on him, that boy would be penniless and homeless."

"He can't be that bad," Helen said.

"He is," Camilla said. "Alex comes up with incredible ideas that make him wealthy, then forgets to invest the money into anything sensible. Don't get me started on his paperwork. Lorna, don't take any nonsense from him. He needs your help and guidance."

"I'll do my best with him." I exchanged an amused glance with Helen. Camilla sounded like a scary mom. "Alex lives here with you?"

"I can't let him have his own place," Camilla said. "Goodness knows what horrors he'd get up to if he wasn't supervised. He'd probably have installed a hot tub in the lounge and given his money to all those sycophants who pretend to be his friends. Or purchased a chain of pizza restaurants so he could get free takeout every night. Helen, you need to put a stop to that bad habit of his. You can't run on junk food."

"It's good you're looking out for him," Helen said. "I'll make sure he has plenty of good food to eat."

"Somebody has to," Camilla said. "Let me show you around."

We grabbed our cases from the trunk and headed for the front door.

As I got closer to the door, I could hear animals snorting and got the scent of farmyard drifting toward me. "Have you got farm animals here?"

"Only Lucy," Camilla said.

"Is she a dog?" I asked.

"No! She's a pig. You'll meet her. She spends most of her time in the house. Alex insists upon it." Camilla shook her head as she pulled the door open. "Sometimes, I think I indulge that boy too much. He loves that pig, though, so I've done something right."

I looked at Helen. A pig in the house! I hoped she was potty trained.

We walked into a vast whitewashed open plan hall, with two doors leading off from the main entrance. There was a staircase to the right, with more chrome and glass fittings. I glimpsed the kitchen at the end of the corridor.

"Right this way." Camilla ran sprightly up the stairs. "I'll show you your rooms, and then you can meet Alex. I've told him you're exactly what he needs. Alex needs a strong steer to keep him on course and not get distracted by his childish pursuits."

"His computer games?" I asked.

"Among other things," Camilla said.

I imagined Alex would be interested in meeting us. I hadn't spoken to him once during the recruitment process, yet we were to be working together every day. I knew he was young, so perhaps he wasn't interested in getting involved in the recruitment side of his business. He must be keen to know who'd be interfering in his life. I hoped we'd get along.

Camilla showed us two immaculately presented cream bedrooms, both with double beds, closets, and dressing tables. "You each have your own attached bathroom. These rooms are entirely private. Neither of you will be disturbed up here."

"The accommodation is perfect," Helen said. "When do I get to see the kitchen?"

"That can be our next stop," Camilla said. "Alex doesn't have the best diet. I'm sure you can tempt him with some wonderful food, though."

"I'll do my best," Helen said. "I've got plenty of ideas for meals."

A blast of rock music shot up the stairs. "Players, choose your weapons," a deep, menacing voice said.

Camilla sighed and shook her head. "It sounds as if Alex is awake."

I raised my eyebrows at Helen. "Does he usually get up so late?"

"My son's a night owl." Camilla led the way back down the stairs and along the hallway. "You will change that. Alex needs to keep more regular hours. People try to contact him about business opportunities, and he's still lying in bed. It doesn't give the right impression."

It didn't sound too bad. I wouldn't mind a lie-in now and again.

Camilla pushed open a set of double doors, and we walked into an enormous lounge. Sitting on the cushion scattered black couch was a young man of about twenty, wearing pajama bottoms, a Metallica T-shirt, and slippers in the shape of dragon claws. In his hand was a game controller.

"Alex! You could have gotten dressed." Camilla hurried over to him. "You knew Lorna and Helen were coming today."

Alex glanced over. He had a pale complexion, which suggested he spent too long inside, staring at a computer screen. "Sorry. It slipped my mind. I'm about to crack level fourteen on Zombie Death Hunters. I've been up most of the night."

"Never mind your ridiculous zombie game," Camilla said. "Meet your new assistant, Lorna."

Alex paused the game and dropped the controller on the couch. He stood and extended a hand. "Hey! It's nice to meet you."

"And you." I shook his hand. "That's quite a computer screen." I gestured to the enormous screen attached to the wall. It must have been at least seventy inches wide.

"It needs to be. I spend most of my time gaming."

Helen shook his hand. "Isn't your business online apps?"

"Some of it is." Alex ran his hands through his bed messy dark hair. "I dabble in loads of things. Computer games being one of them. To be the best, you have to know your competition. I've been playing this every day for a month. Do either of you play?"

"I'm more of a board games kind of girl," Helen said.

Alex raised his eyebrows at me. "What about you? You need to be good at games if you're to be my assistant. Have you ever played Zombie Death Hunters?"

"I can't say I have." I stared at the screen, where a frozen, salivating zombie looked like it was about to reach through and eat us all. Violent video games weren't my thing. There was no way Alex would get me to play anything like that. Paperwork and the tax returns I could handle. I wouldn't spend hours staring at a screen fighting imaginary enemies.

Alex shrugged and shuffled back toward the couch. "I'll show you some insider tricks. Most of the games are easy, once you know your way around them. It takes time. You need to immerse yourself in them to become a master."

"Yes, yes. I'm sure these young ladies are fascinated by all the hours you waste slumped on that couch," Camilla said. "That's not why they're here. They're here to sort you out and make sure the business is in a fit shape. Don't forget, you're our main breadwinner now."

Alex ducked his head. "As if I could forget that. You tell me all the time."

"We'll have none of that." Camilla tutted and shook her head. "It's not as if we have a choice in the matter."

I was going to ask what she meant, when a snuffling noise caught my attention.

Flipper's ears pricked up. He took a few steps toward the door.

A pig the size of a small dog wandered into the room, its nose on the wooden floorboards. That must be Lucy. She was so focused on snuffling out a treat on the floor that she didn't notice us.

Flipper gave me a startled look before stepping cautiously toward the pig.

"Lucy! I wondered where you were." Alex hurried over to the pig and wrapped his arms around her. She gently snuffled her snout against his stubble. "It's way past your breakfast time. You must be starving."

Camilla tutted again. "Welcome to my bizarre family, ladies. This is Lucy."

Alex looked up from scrubbing his fingers across Lucy's back. "You can pet her if you like. She's tame. I've had her since she was tiny. I got her as a gift from a friend. Lucy thinks I'm her dad. Well, maybe her big brother. I'm not sure, really." He looked at Flipper, who studied Lucy intently. "Is your dog okay around pigs?"

"He's never been bothered by them before." I kept a hand on Flipper's head, just in case he took a bit too much interest in Lucy and scared her. "This is the first time he's met one in a house. In fact, it's the first time I've met one inside, as well."

"Lucy's house-trained." Alex stood and wandered back to the couch, Lucy following behind, wagging her curly tail. "If the weather's terrible, I bring her in a giant litter tray, and she uses that. She's never once made a mess. You have nothing to worry about."

I knelt and held my hand out to Lucy. She looked at me with her small black eyes before walking over and giving my hand a snuffle.

Lucy turned her attention to Flipper, and they touched noses. So far, so good. Maybe Flipper would think Lucy was some kind of odd looking dog, and they could make friends. It would be nice for him to have company while he was here. He always missed Jessie when they were apart.

"Lucy's a good judge of character," Alex said with a smile. "I can tell she likes you."

"She's sweet," I said. "And it looks like she wants to make friends with Flipper."

"I hope they get along," Alex said, a game controller already in his hand. "Pigs are sociable animals. She gets lonely hanging out here with me. I try to keep her entertained; you'll find pig toys around the house, balls and treat things. She also loves playing tug with an old bit of towel. Don't throw it out or wash it if you find it lying around. Having a four-legged friend around will be a good thing for her."

"Let's hope so," I said. Alex seemed nice. Maybe a little too obsessed with computer games, but decent enough. And, anyone who loved animals was okay in my book.

"Let me show you the rest of the house. Then you can spend time with Alex," Camilla said, who'd been walking around the room, picking up discarded shoes and pig toys.

"I'll be hours on this game," Alex said. "If there's a chance of some toast and tea, I wouldn't say no."

"You get your own toast, young man," Camilla said.

"I don't mind making toast for Alex," Helen said. "After all, I am the new house cook."

"No! He needs to know the rules and stick to them," Camilla said. "He must become more self-sufficient."

Alex gave an apologetic shrug before his gaze flicked to the screen.

"You can play on your computer for half an hour," Camilla said. "Then it must be switched off and you spend time with Lorna, showing her what needs to be done."

Alex grumbled under his breath as we left the room. It must be hard having such a domineering mother. It looked like he needed taking care of, though. I could imagine, if Camilla wasn't here, Alex would spend all day glued to the couch, his eyes turning square as he killed his thousandth zombie of the day.

We looked around the rest of the house, discovering a dining room, separate sitting room, study, games room, and finally the kitchen.

Helen hurried in and looked around. It was an open plan room, with an enormous island in the center, covered in an expensive marble slab. It looked like the family enjoyed their kitchen gadgets. There was everything from the latest coffeemaker to a top of the range juicer.

"I hope this will do," Camilla said. "Neither Alex nor I are adept in the kitchen. I'm usually too busy to stop and cook a meal. Alex eats anything that comes out of a packet. Now you're here, Helen, we hope that will change."

"This all looks perfect," Helen said.

"Neither of us like fancy food," Camilla said. "Good wholesome food, that's all we require."

"My meals are always wholesome. But I also do good desserts."

"We only eat dessert on the weekend." Camilla patted her flat stomach. "It's important not to let yourself go."

The joy in Helen's eyes dimmed. She liked dessert at every meal, breakfast included. Maybe this wouldn't be quite the joyful cooking experience she'd hoped for.

"I'll leave you both to it," Camilla said. "Get yourselves settled in. And, Lorna, be sure to spend time with Alex this evening. Don't mind if he complains about you interfering with his computer games. Those dreadful zombies will still be there when you've finished. The end of the world won't occur because Alex isn't staring a zombie down and blasting it in the head with an AK-47."

Camilla left the kitchen, leaving me wondering just how tricky it would be to get Alex to do any actual work.

Helen had a swift look through the cupboards. She shut the last one and turned. "There's not much here. Camilla was right about wanting nothing but plain, boring food."

"Didn't she actually say clean and wholesome food?" I grinned. "That can't be a bad thing."

"There's no butter or cream in the fridge," Helen said. "How am I supposed to make brownies with no butter?"

"Can't you make a fat free version?" I suggested. "Didn't you try a recipe once that used applesauce instead of fat?"

Helen's nose wrinkled. "Then it wouldn't be one of my legendary brownies. It would be a clean and wholesome brownie."

"Which sounds about perfect for this family. Camilla seems very proper about things."

Helen grimaced. "Even their granola said it was low-fat on the packaging. I'll have a hard job making fun meals for this family. There's not much you can do with fat free spread and a stick of celery."

"I'm sure you'll come up with amazing meals." We left the kitchen and walked back along the hall.

I paused and looked in on Alex, who was staring at the computer screen as he fired at a horde of oncoming zombies.

Flipper poked his head in the door. It looked as if he was seeking his new friend, Lucy. He nudged me with his nose and whined.

A shiver ran down my spine and a familiar lightheaded feeling hit me. I looked more carefully around the room. As I did so, I saw a pale haze hovering next to Alex.

I stared at it, and the ghost of a young man appeared.

Chapter 3

Grabbing hold of Helen's elbow, I hurried us away from the door and up the stairs to our bedrooms, Flipper right at my heel, keeping an ever-watchful eye on me.

"What's wrong?" Helen asked, once I'd shut the bedroom door behind me.

"Alex has a friend," I said

"I doubt he has many of those," Helen said. "These gaming addicts spend a lot of time on their own. Maybe he's a bit socially deficient."

"No! That's not what I mean."

"Lucy the pig?"

"No! Not a living kind of friend."

Helen's eyebrows shot up. "A ghost friend?"

"Yes. He was standing right next to Alex, watching him play."

Helen sank onto my bed. Flipper hopped up beside her. "I wonder who he could be?"

"They looked about the same age."

"Was there any family resemblance? Maybe Alex had a brother who died."

"Not that I could see," I said. "He had lighter hair and wore glasses. He didn't look all that happy, though."

"You'd hardly be happy if you were dead," Helen said.

"I don't know. Some of the ghosts we meet aren't unhappy. This one had a really sad expression on his face, though."

"It could be he was sad because he can't play that dreadful computer game with Alex. Maybe he was as much of a geek as Alex," Helen said.

"I don't think Alex is a geek," I said, "a bit of a loner, maybe, and obsessed with his computer. His obsession has made him wealthy. There's a lot of money in computer games and apps."

"That sounds geeky to me," Helen said.

"Don't tell me you wouldn't like to make a living out of doing something you love."

She grinned at me. "I already do. But I don't get obsessed with it. I have a life outside of work."

"You have Gunner," I said.

"I have a lot more than Gunner." Helen's cheeks glowed pink. "Having a boyfriend isn't my sole purpose in life."

I smiled at her comment. Ever since I'd known Helen, she'd been obsessed with getting married and settling down. Now that it looked like she might achieve it, she was trying far too hard to hide that fact. "What else do you have?"

"I have you. I make my own clothes. I love to cook and eat what I cook. There's plenty going on in my life, thank you very much."

"Fine. We've confirmed you're not a geek. That doesn't help us figure out who this ghost could be."

"Maybe Alex had a boyfriend?" Helen suggested. "That would be sad to lose someone at such a young age."

"They could have been school friends rather than partners," I said.

Helen looked around the neat bedroom. "It's hard to get a sense of the people in this house. Usually, you can tell by the décor what a person's like. All I'm seeing is a lot of cream or white. A complete lack of color. That suggests a lack of personality."

"The house is lacking a feminine touch. From what we've seen of Camilla, she rules this place with an iron rod. She must decide on all the decorating, so we're seeing her personality in the house, rather than Alex's."

"Everything is tidy and has an allocated space," Helen said. "It's very precise, apart from the lounge, which must be where Alex spends his time. That room is a car crash."

"We can't all love florals and patterned wallpaper," I said. "This is a lovely house." Helen was right, though; it was incredibly neat and ordered.

There was a knock at the bedroom door. I opened it to find a tall, pale girl standing outside. She was dressed head to toe in black, and her long dark hair was completely straight, hanging almost to her waist. Her eyes were lined with black kohl, making her skin look even paler.

"Since mother didn't bother to introduce us, I thought I'd better do it myself. I'm Eva, Alex's sister."

Camilla hadn't mentioned having another child. "It's nice to meet you." I introduced myself and then Helen and Flipper.

"Don't worry. I don't expect you've heard anything about me." Eva flicked her gaze along the corridor. "I'm something of the black sheep of the family." She waved her hand at her outfit. "Quite literally at the moment."

"Maybe you could try navy if you prefer dark colors," Helen said as she walked over. "Black can be very... draining on the complexion."

Eva carefully looked over Helen's outfit. "I know what I like. I don't always wear black. Thanks for the tip, though."

"Do you live here as well?" I asked, sensing Eva's tension at Helen's tactless fashion advice.

"I will until I can get enough money to get out," Eva said. "I'm not a fan of all this flashy show of wealth. They only got this place because Mom insisted on it after Alex's business made so much money. Mom likes nothing more than to show off everything we've got. There's three of us living here and eight bedrooms. We rarely have guests. What are we supposed to do with all the empty rooms?"

As I carefully checked out Eva's clothing, I could tell it was designer and tailored to fit her. She might protest about all the wealth, but it looked like she didn't mind spending it. "I was just saying what a great house this is."

Eva shrugged. "It's okay." She looked at Helen. "What time will dinner be ready?"

"Oh! Am I cooking tonight?" Helen asked.

"Mom said you'll do the cooking for us from now on." Eva tilted her head. "Isn't that why you're here?"

"Yes! It is." Helen flapped her hands in front of her. "I didn't realize I'd be cooking tonight! I must check my recipes and then look in the cupboards to see if I've got everything I need. I wanted to make my first dinner something special."

"Don't worry about showing off to us," Eva said. "The food around here is usually instant and comes out of a packet. I eat out a lot. Or cereal, that's good. I like Thai. Can you make Thai food?"

"Absolutely! But not tonight." Helen looked distraught.

"Whatever you make, I'm sure it will be fine." Eva gestured along the corridor. "Have you seen the kitchen yet?"

"We have," I said, gently pushing Helen out of the way as she flapped around, muttering under her breath about some spice I'd never heard of. "Helen will make you all something great."

Eva watched Helen panic for a few more seconds before shrugging again. "I'm heading down there if you want to come. I can show you where all the stuff is kept."

"Yes! Maybe I missed some of your supplies. Let me grab my recipes." Helen dashed to her own room.

Eva frowned and dabbed her fingers against her carefully drawn black eyebrows. "Is she always like that?"

"It has been known."

"She should chill out. Stress is a killer."

"So I've heard."

Eva looked at me. "I like your aura."

I looked down at my tan pants. "That's not the brand I'm wearing."

Eva rolled her eyes. "I mean your *aura*." She spread her arms in a circle. "You give off a good vibe."

"That's nice to know." I wasn't sure I believed in auras, but then a lot of people didn't believe in ghosts and I saw them all the time so what did I know. "What does my aura show you?"

"You're open-minded," Eva said. "You like to help people. You have a lot of silver mixed in there. That shows your cosmic mind is also open."

"I hope that doesn't mean aliens will make contact any time soon. I'm not keen on being whisked away by little green men."

Eva snorted. "If that were to happen, they wouldn't be little or green. And there's no way men are smart enough to conquer space. Women will be the ones to do that."

"So, I need to look out for large, alien-like women creeping through my window?"

Eva frowned. "Maybe you're not so open-minded."

"What about Flipper's aura?" I looked down at him.

She wrinkled her nose. "Animals don't have auras."

Of course they didn't. Why didn't I know that?

"I've got the recipes." Helen ran out of her room, her treasured recipe file in her hands. "Let's go make dinner."

Eva nodded and led the way down the stairs.

"This wasn't what I had planned for my first night," Helen muttered as we followed Eva.

"You don't say."

"I was going to do a three-course extravaganza to wow everyone. I'll be lucky if I can make one decent dish."

"Your food is always amazing. There's nothing to worry about."

"There is! I want to broaden my skills. It'll make me more employable."

"You do fine for work."

"But sometimes, I want to offer more. You know I like to keep busy."

That was an understatement. A bored Helen was a dangerous Helen. She needed to keep her hands busy and her mind occupied. Otherwise, she meddled too much in my business.

Eva held the door open for us as we walked into the kitchen. "The pantry's at the end. We keep herbs, spices, and dried stuff in there."

"That's a good start." Helen walked over and opened the door. "Is there a food delivery coming soon?"

"Nope. Not for another week," Eva said.

Helen pulled out six packets of chicken flavored noodles and a tin of beans. "This is all you've got in your dried goods pantry?"

"There are the spices as well." Eva wandered over to the pantry. "I put cayenne pepper on my noodles. We always have plenty of tomato sauce too. That makes anything taste better."

"Well, that's... inventive." Helen placed the noodles back in the pantry. "What can I use in the fridge?"

I followed her, Flipper also taking an interest when he saw the fridge door open.

"This is a bit better." Helen pulled out a carton of eggs, some peppers, and an onion. "I can do something with this."

"I don't like eggs," Eva said.

"Oh, well, maybe you'll have to stick to noodles for tonight," Helen said. "Does your brother like eggs?"

"I think so. We rarely eat together. He's always stuck in front of his computer."

"Does he have friends over to play often?" I asked. Maybe Eva could shed light on who Alex's ghost friend was.

"Sometimes. Piers and Harriet hang out here a lot." Eva picked at the hem of her shirt. "They're not much fun to play with, though."

"Do you play on the computer with Alex?"

"Sometimes. I have a good setup in my bedroom."

"You mean, you play together but in separate rooms?"

"Sure, why not? It means I don't have to put up with his fist pumping and hyperactive behavior if he beats me. We fight less if we aren't in the same room. Plus, if Piers is around, I don't have to put up with him staring down my top all the time. That guy is such a sleaze." She adjusted the modest black vest top she wore under her black shirt.

"You mentioned earlier that you don't always wear black," I said. "Is there a reason you're wearing it now?"

Eva looked at her clothes. "Sure. I'm wearing it because I'm in mourning for Gregory."

Chapter 4

"Who's Gregory?" Helen looked up from her frantic beating of a bowl of eggs.

"He was Alex's best friend. He died recently." Eva looked around the kitchen, worrying a hangnail on the side of her thumb.

"You were close?" I asked.

"Sort of. I liked him. We hung out a lot and talked about computer games. He was cool."

"I'm sorry to hear he's dead." Could this be our ghost friend? "Do you mind telling me how he died?"

"I'm surprised you haven't heard. The story made the national news. It was so weird."

I shook my head. "What happened?"

"Gregory was shot by a drone in the middle of the night."

I opened my mouth, but nothing came out.

Helen stopped beating the eggs. The whisk she held out dripped raw egg onto the tiles. "Wait! I heard about that. Didn't the drone malfunction? It was being tested at a private base. The drone went rogue. Some guy ended up in its firing line."

"That's pretty much what happened," Eva said. "That base you're talking about is five miles from here. You can hear the planes go overhead sometimes. It's supposed to be top secret, but everyone living around here knows what they get up to."

"What was Gregory doing out at night at a top-secret airbase?" Helen asked.

"He'd just left here," Eva said. "He'd often work through the night with Alex when they were planning their next big thing. Gregory didn't drive. He biked everywhere. He's got an apartment near the base. He was taking a shortcut through the fields when the drone targeted him."

"They're testing dangerous weapons at this base?"

Helen started to beat the eggs again. "They must be, if that's what happened to Gregory."

Eva nodded. "He was Alex's friend. They met as kids and went to the same school. They were such geeks together, but so smart that they got away with it. They won every school science prize going. Both of them got full scholarships funded by private companies to study computer science at Oxford."

"They went to university together?" I asked.

"Gregory went. Alex dropped out after the first year. He reckoned he could teach himself better than some out-of-date professor with a bow tie and patches on his jacket elbows. He was probably right." Eva gestured at the kitchen. "Alex is the reason we live in this huge place. He paid for it in cash after his dating app took off and he sold it for mega bucks."

For someone so young, that was impressive. In fact, to have paid off your mortgage before you retired was a miracle. "Were Alex and Gregory in business together?"

"Yes. They came up with a ton of great ideas," Eva said. "Alex had a target of thinking up ten new ideas every day. He said if he kept doing that, at least one would be good. And, as much as I hate to praise my giant-brained brother, most were decent. He could have sold a hundred. Gregory was the details guy. He'd take one of Alex's ideas and run with it, test out the market, see if people liked it. He'd profile the ideas, and they'd decide which ones to take forward. They worked well together. Gregory was a good guy. He got on with most people."

"He sounds nice," I said. "You must miss him."

Eva's bottom lip jutted out. "I sometimes think he didn't know I existed. He was always thinking about a new idea or a new trick on a game he played. It's why I got into gaming. I thought he'd notice me if I stepped into his world."

"I bet he noticed you." I felt a twinge of sympathy for Eva. It must be hard when the guy you were into barely noticed you were alive.

Eva glanced at me. "I knew you had the kind of aura that made people open up to you. You have a way about you that makes me want to talk. I never want to talk."

Helen tapped her whisk against the edge of the bowl. "Lorna has an aura?"

Eva nodded, and her gaze ran over Helen. "So do you."

Helen's blue eyes widened. "What does my aura say?"

Eva pursed her lips. "You have lots of red in your aura."

"That's good?"

"It means you're very... adventurous."

Helen smiled. "I like the sound of that."

Eva shot me a glance. "Yeah, lots of red is great. I'd better go. I look forward to dinner." She left us in the kitchen.

I pulled out my phone and searched the meaning of a red aura. "Hmmm. Maybe red isn't the best thing to have in your aura."

"Eva said it was." Helen looked up from chopping an onion. "Why? What have you discovered?"

I repressed a grin. "Having a red aura does mean you're adventurous in areas such as food and travel."

"Both true. What else?"

"You have a strong body and mind." I kept scrolling, trying to find more positive things about Helen's aura. "And you're generous with your energy, helping others when you can."

"Which is all great." Helen's eyes narrowed. "Go on, what else?"

"You're sexually adventurous and quick to anger. You tend to lose your temper at the smallest thing."

"What rubbish! I never lose my temper."

I raised my eyebrows. "You can get a bit... flappy in stressful situations."

"I never flap!"

My gaze went to the file of recipes. "Okay, you're a picture of serenity and calm."

Helen crinkled her nose. "I'll admit to being passionate about things. But as for the sexual stuff, that's nonsense. I mean, I'm not a prude, but a lady must have her limits."

Flipper nudged me with his nose and gave a gentle whine.

The surrounding air chilled, and Gregory appeared. He was a tall, thin guy, with large blue eyes and a gloomy expression on his face.

"Let's forget about your aura," I said. "We've got more important things to focus on."

"I happen to think my aura is very important," Helen said.

"Auras aren't even a real thing," I said. "I was humoring Eva. Besides, we have company."

"Gregory?" Helen looked around the room. "Or does he prefer Greg? I think that's a lovely name."

Gregory looked over at Helen and nodded.

"Greg it is," I said. "I'm sorry to hear about what happened to you. Eva was just telling us about the drone accident."

"Was it an accident?" Helen asked. "Is that why you're still here, Greg?"

Greg nodded.

"You think the drone attacked you?" I asked him. "How do you know?"

He mimed playing on a game controller.

"You can't have been controlling the drone," I said. "You'd have hardly shot yourself."

He scowled and shook his head.

"Somebody else was controlling the drone," Helen said. "It's one of those new trends, isn't it, kids going to the park with their drones and spying on the neighbors."

"This wasn't a kid's toy by the sounds of it," I said. "Any drone used by the military has got to be hard core."

Greg nodded, before running around the kitchen, shooting worried looks over his shoulder.

Helen shivered and wrapped her arms around herself. "What's he up to? It's getting freezing in here."

"I think he's showing me he was chased by the drone," I said.

"It could have gone wrong," Helen said. "Greg, slow down! It'll get too cold in here and ruin my soufflé."

Greg slowed and looked at me.

"The first time I saw you, you appeared next to Alex. Does he have something to do with your death?"

Greg shook his head quickly.

"You didn't fall out over something?" I asked.

He shook his head again.

"Okay, so if you don't think Alex was involved, what about Eva?"

Greg's eyebrows shot up.

"She seems fond of you," I said. "Were you close?"

Greg's mouth fell open. He looked at the doorway Eva had walked through. He drifted toward it and stopped. Returning to my side, he tilted his head.

"What's he doing?" Helen asked.

I smiled. "Looking dumbstruck. You and Eva weren't an item? She's not a jealous girlfriend who gunned you down with a drone?"

Greg's image wavered, before vanishing.

I let out a sigh. "I'll have to take that as a no. He's gone."

The kitchen door opened. Camilla walked in and looked at Helen's cooking efforts. "I wanted to check on dinner. I hope you don't mind cooking at such short notice."

"It's not a problem." Helen pasted a bright smile on her face. "It'll be simple food tonight. I'll make you something lovely once I've been shopping."

"That's all we need," Camilla said. "I'd suggest we lay the table in the dining room, but it's impossible to pry Alex away from his games when he's engrossed in a mission. I sometimes have to resort to cutting the power to get him to pay attention. We might as well eat in the lounge. Otherwise, you'll never see him."

"Dinner won't be long," I said.

Camilla nodded. "Jolly good." She sniffed the air as if trying to figure out what dinner would be, and then left.

"Eat in the lounge!" Helen said, the second Camilla had gone. "Is she going to make us sit with dinner on our laps while we watch Alex play games?"

"It sounds like it," I said.

"We can't eat soufflé off lap trays."

"It might make it taste better."

"You're no help," Helen grumbled as she continued to attack the vegetables she was chopping.

She was right, I was no help in the kitchen, but I could help Greg. If someone had shot him, then I wanted to know who and why. I needed to find out more about this family and just what had happened to my sad-faced ghost.

Chapter 5

Half an hour later, Helen's cheese soufflés were ready, along with Cayenne spiced noodles for Eva. She'd also made a balsamic glazed salad to go alongside it, with the wilting contents of the salad drawer.

"Go and tell everyone dinner is ready," she said. "See if you can get them to the table."

I walked into the lounge, with Flipper by my side. My thoughts were still on Greg and what had happened to him. As I entered the lounge, a loud explosion rang out, and I ducked.

Alex jumped to his feet and punched the air. "Take that, you flesh eating scum."

"I hate to interrupt anything important," I said as I stood up straight and smoothed down my hair, "but dinner is ready."

"Is it that time already?" Alex checked the wall clock. "I guess we can eat."

"Shall we have it at the table?"

Alex was already slumping back on the couch, the game controller in one hand. "No way. Bring it through here. We always eat in the lounge."

I pressed my lips together and returned to the kitchen. Helen wouldn't be happy to hear that. Personally, I didn't mind the occasional dinner in front of the TV. It was a nice way to relax.

Four soufflés sat neatly in their bowls as I entered the kitchen. "Shall I take these through?"

"To the table?" Helen gave me a hopeful look.

I shook my head. "Boss's orders. He wants to eat in the lounge."

"For goodness sake." Helen grabbed three plates and expertly balanced them on her hands. "You lead the way. If Alex asks for tomato sauce with his soufflé, it'll end up on his head."

"I think that's Eva's condiment of choice." I walked back to the lounge, carrying the rest of the food, and found Alex had been joined by Camilla and Eva.

They both took their plates of food happily enough. When Helen offered Alex his soufflé, he frowned and shook his head. "I don't like fancy food."

"This isn't fancy," Helen said. "It's eggs and cheese."

"It's not my thing," Alex said. "I'm sure your food is lovely, though. Any chance I could have instant noodles like Eva? Or beans on toast?"

Helen's mouth opened and closed several times. "Beans on toast?"

"It's my favorite meal," Alex said. "I eat it almost every night. I change the flavors by having different sorts of noodles on the side. They come in all different varieties. I like the Chinese Chicken ones the best, but they always sell out. Whatever you can find in the cupboard will be fine."

Helen's mouth flapped again.

I grabbed the unwanted soufflé from her and gently pushed her back toward the door. "She'll make a note of your favorite noodles for next time."

Alex nodded, already distracted by the game he was in the middle of.

Helen scowled at me. "Right. Noodles it is." She stomped out of the room.

Flipper looked eagerly at the unwanted soufflé in my hand. I discreetly gave him a small bit but didn't want him to have too much because the richness could upset his stomach.

"This is really good," Eva said, half of her noodles already gone.

I sat in an armchair and made a start on my food. "Helen's a great cook."

The doorbell rang, and Alex glanced up. "That's probably Piers and Harriet."

Eva groaned. "Don't they have homes of their own?"

Alex shrugged. "They like hanging out here. Can you let them in?"

"They're your friends."

"I'm in the middle of an important grudge match. If I leave, I die."

"Important in whose world?" Eva sneered.

"Children! There's no need to bicker," Camilla said. "Eva, answer the door."

"Alex should do it. He's just playing one of his dumb computer games," Eva protested.

"Go. Now." Camilla's tone was not to be argued with.

Eva stuffed a huge pile of noodles into her mouth before stomping into the hallway. "They're not even my friends." She returned a moment later and slumped into an armchair in the corner, her food forgotten.

A tall, slender blonde in skin tight, dark jeans and a fitted T-shirt walked in. She squealed when she saw Alex, ran over, and flung her arms around him. "I've missed you." She planted a kiss on his cheek.

Alex struggled out of her embrace. "In a minute, babe. I'm on an important mission."

The blonde pouted. "I'm your important mission."

"You will be in just a second."

The blonde looked around, her pale blue eyes narrowing when she saw me. "Who are you?"

"I'm Lorna," I said. "Alex's new assistant."

"I'm Alex's girlfriend, Harriet Fawcett." She thumped Alex's arm. "You should have said if you needed an assistant. I can help you. I'd be a great personal assistant. I can see to *all* of your needs."

"Lorna's not that kind of assistant." Camilla finished her last mouthful of salad and neatly placed her knife and fork together. "She's here to make sure Alex's business is successful and all the paperwork is in order."

Harriet pouted again. "I can do that. Doing paperwork must be easy. He didn't need to hire her."

"Yes, he did." Camilla picked up her empty plate and stood. "It can't all be computer games and fun. He needs to think about his long-term future and who will be in it." Her icy gaze settled on Harriet. "I'll leave you all to it. Enjoy your evening. And, Alex, don't forget to spend time with Lorna going over her work duties."

Alex waved a hand in the air as his mom left the room.

Harriet studied me in silence before turning back to Alex. "Well, I guess she'll do. She's not your type, so I don't need to be jealous." She shot me a cold look before circling Alex's arm with both hands and tugging on his elbow. "Finish your silly game. I'm already bored."

I resisted the urge to remind her what my name was. Being called *she* all the time was grating on my nerves.

Alex shot Harriet an irritated look. "This isn't silly. This is important. I'm playing Mickey."

Harriet groaned and slumped onto the couch as if realizing she'd been defeated.

I finished my food and shuffled closer toward the screen. "Who's Mickey?"

"Mickey Kill is a legend." A tall, dark-haired guy stood in the doorway, leaning against the door jamb. At first glance, he was attractive, but there was a coldness in his eyes that set me on edge.

"Mickey Kill is an idiot," Harriet said. "He takes up far too much of Alex's time."

The dark-haired guy strolled into the room. "I'm Piers Torrington, Alex's best friend." He raised his eyebrows at me.

"I'm Lorna Shadow. His new personal assistant."

Piers nodded. "I remember Alex mentioning something about his mom getting him an assistant. She's worried he can't look after himself."

"I do fine on my own." Alex shot me a guilty look. "Although, maybe I could do with a hand with some of the paperwork now and again."

"You don't need to worry about the paperwork." Piers settled on the couch on the other side of Alex. "All you need to do is come up with brilliant business ideas to make your next few million."

"I do my best," Alex said.

"What's your latest idea?" he asked.

Alex shrugged. "I haven't thought up anything good for a while."

"Then you need to," Piers said. "Your latest hot app will be an old app in a month's time. If you don't innovate, you go out of date quickly in this business."

"What is it that you do?" I asked Piers.

He smirked. "This and that."

"Piers lives off his parents," Eva muttered from the corner.

He glared at her. "My business dealings are none of your concern. Don't you have a graveyard to haunt? You're certainly dressed for it."

Eva glared at him. "I'm in mourning."

Piers shook his head. "Mourning your lack of style and inability to find a boyfriend."

"Piers is an entrepreneur," Harriet simpered. "He's brilliant."

"Thank you, gorgeous." Piers smiled at her and winked.

Helen walked in with a tray of instant noodles and beans on toast. "Here's your dinner."

Alex's face brightened, and he paused the game. "Brilliant. Any chance you can make some for Piers and Harriet?"

Piers's gaze raked over Helen. His tongue traced across his lips. "I like the sound of that."

"Nothing for me," Harriet said. "I need to watch my weight. Alex is taking me to a movie premier soon. I must fit into my new white tube dress."

"Beans on toast for one it is." Helen sighed, turned on her heel, and left.

Alex tucked into his food, one eye still on the game.

"I can take over if you'd like," Eva said.

"There's no need," Alex said. "I got this."

"Mickey Kill is getting agitated." Eva gestured to the screen, where a series of short messages were pinging up. *Are you giving up? Have I beaten you? You a loser? It's a fight to the death. Are you scared?*

I watched the text scroll down the screen. "This Mickey Kill doesn't sound like a nice guy." Mind you, neither did Piers, and I was sitting in the same room as him.

"He's just playing," Alex said. "We're as bad as each other."

"It would be different if you were face-to-face," Eva said. "You know what these gamers are like. It's all bravado and show when they're hidden behind a screen. Get them talking to each other, and I bet they wouldn't say boo to a mouse."

"That's not true," Alex said. "Besides, you have to play the game. Mickey Kill plays some of the best game around. I can handle his trash talk so long as we can play together."

"I could beat him if I made the effort," Piers said. "He wouldn't be a match for me."

"You can take him on if you like," Alex said. "But you're not using my game credits to do so. It's taken me all week to build up to this level."

Piers yawned and stretched his arms over his head. "It's hardly a challenge for me."

Alex snorted. "Yeah, right. Mickey Kill would obliterate you in seconds."

I can beat anyone. The message on the screen from Mickey Kill was eerily accurate.

I blinked and stared at it. It was as if he was listening to our conversation and had just heard Piers.

Alex scooped up the last of his beans before setting his plate on the floor. "Let's play."

For the next twenty minutes, I watched spellbound, as Alex slaughtered zombies in a variety of inventive ways. He was competing with Mickey Kill to get the most zombie slays. I flinched as Alex sliced off various limbs from a slow-moving zombie and used them to beat another around the head.

I felt old. When did computer games get so violent? I used to like the ones where you'd chase balls around the screen, jump onto different platforms, and catch magic coins in the sky. If games had been like this when I was a kid, I'd have been scarred for life.

Helen returned with Piers's food, ignoring the lecherous looks he gave her as she handed him the plate.

"Are you staying?" I asked her.

She looked at the screen and grimaced. "I'm busy in the kitchen." Helen scooped up the empty plates and made a hasty retreat.

Eva perched on the edge of my seat and leaned over. "This was Gregory's favorite game. He used to love to play it with Alex."

Alex glanced up. "He did enjoy it. We had a lot of fun with this game."

"I could have beaten Greg at this," Piers sneered. "He wasn't all that good. He didn't have the killer instinct."

"He did. He was brilliant," Eva said. "You never played with him because you knew he'd always beat you."

"That's rubbish," Piers said. "I was out of his league. Besides, he never asked me to play."

"Because he was Alex's friend, not yours," Eva said. She leaned even closer and lowered her voice. "Gregory and Piers didn't get along."

"We were all mates," Alex said.

"Whatever you say, buddy." Piers slapped Alex on the shoulder. "We had fun together."

"Gregory wasn't just great at this game," Eva whispered. "He was the brains behind everything Alex did."

I looked up at her. "Like what?"

"Their business success was down to Gregory. If it weren't for him, Alex would be sitting in a single room apartment playing this game on his own. He wouldn't have the likes of Harriet and Piers hanging around trying to get a handout."

I glanced at Harriet and Piers. They were both cheering Alex on as he killed more zombies. Their friendships looked genuine enough, but maybe they were hiding something. Maybe they could be here because there was money to be had.

"Alex is a sucker," Eva muttered. "He can be a real idiot. I've told him not to trust those two, but he won't listen to me."

"What are you muttering about?" Harriet glared at Eva. "If you keep talking, you'll distract Alex from his game."

"She's not the only one," Alex murmured. "I could do with some peace."

"Why don't I join in?" Piers went to grab the second game controller sitting on the coffee table.

Alex scooped it up and tucked it under his arm. "It's me and Mickey Kill tonight. We've been playing all day. I'm not going to give up now. It wouldn't be fair to bring a second player in on my side."

Piers shrugged. "Suit yourself. I'll go grab some beers from the kitchen, shall I?"

"I'll have a soft drink," Alex said. "I need to keep a clear head for this game."

"One beer won't hurt." Piers shoved Alex in the shoulder.

"I need to stay alert. Maybe I should have a coffee, instead?"

"You're such a wimp." Piers jumped off the couch and headed into the hallway.

"Do you see how Piers treats Alex?" Eva whispered. "He's always like that around him. He's always picking on him and trying to undermine his confidence."

I glanced over to see Harriet fiddling with Alex's hair while he leaned away from her. "Why would he do that if they're friends?"

"That's my point," Eva said. "They aren't, not really."

Harriet glared at Eva. "If you two are going to keep whispering, then you must leave. Alex needs to concentrate."

"They're fine," Alex said. "I can't hear them."

"Neither can I, but I can hear them mumbling. It's annoying," Harriet said. "We're all friends here. There's no need to keep secrets."

Eva snorted and stood. "I'm bored, anyway. I'll catch you two lovebirds later." She gave me a knowing nod before leaving the lounge.

Feeling awkward about being the third wheel sitting with Alex and Harriet as she pawed him, I made my excuses and headed to the kitchen.

As I got to the door with Flipper, I heard voices on the other side. One of them was Helen's. She wasn't sounding happy.

I shoved open the door to find Piers standing far too close to Helen, who was backed up against the kitchen island.

Piers looked up as I came in and took a step back, giving me a sly grin as he did so. "I was just getting to know your friend, thanking her for the beans on toast she so kindly made me."

Helen scowled at Piers. "You can keep your thanks to yourself."

"There's no need to be like that." Piers grabbed the cans of beer off the kitchen island. "I was just being friendly."

"I don't need that kind of friendly from you."

Piers shrugged as he walked past me. "It's your loss. You're too old for me, anyway."

I watched the door shut and then turned to Helen. "Was he trying it on with you?"

"Yes! What a disgusting little creep. He was acting as if I should be grateful for his attention. And, as if I'm too old for him! Not that I'd want him. He smells of cheap cologne and beans."

I sank onto a chair and propped my chin on my hand. "This family is weird."

"You're telling me," Helen said. "Anyone who prefers instant noodles and beans on toast over my cooking has to have something wrong with them."

"Most of your soufflés got eaten," I said. "I thought mine was lovely. Flipper enjoyed his as well."

"Flipper always enjoys my food." Helen switched on the kettle. "It's time for hot chocolate."

"And, it's time we figured out exactly what happened to our ghostly friend, Greg."

Chapter 6

The hot chocolate was made, and I was working my way through a plate of double chocolate chip cookies with Helen.

"I'm not sure about this place," I said. "Alex doesn't want me here. I can't work with him if he doesn't want me around. It will make everything awkward."

"I don't think Alex will be a problem," Helen said. "Simply do what his mom does and boss him about. He responds to that. It's all his hangers on and his weird sister who worry me."

"I don't think Eva is weird."

"She told me I was a sexual deviant. That's weird."

I smiled. "Eva said you were adventurous. There's a big difference. Or is there something you've been hiding from me?"

Helen broke apart a cookie and dumped a piece into her hot chocolate before sucking the chocolatey foam off. "I still think she's a bit strange. She's mourning a dead guy who didn't even know she was alive."

"Haven't you ever experienced unrequited love?"

"Never! Well, I thought the lead singer from Hot Rod would marry me. But I was eight years old when I had that fantasy."

"Well, Eva hasn't been so lucky. It looks like she had a crush on Greg and he didn't even notice she was around. That's got to hurt. Now he's dead, she'll never get the chance to tell him how she felt."

Helen shrugged. "If she didn't mope around in so much black, Eva might stand more of a chance with guys."

I shook my head at Helen's lack of sympathy. "We can't all be as lucky in love as you are."

"Maybe Eva had something to do with Greg's death," Helen said. "She could have declared her interest in him, and he rejected her. That's a good motive for wanting someone dead. All this mourning nonsense is a cover."

"It's possible," I said. "I get the impression she really liked him."

"That's even more of a reason," Helen said. "Greg told her there was no way they could be together, and she saw red and attacked him."

"By stealing a top-secret military drone, learning to fly it, and then shooting Greg? There are grounds for pre-meditation there."

"We have no idea what Eva's hobbies are," Helen said. "She could be great at flying drones."

"I'm not so sure," I said. "I wonder about Alex, but Greg seemed convinced he had nothing to do with it."

"What about creepy Piers?" Helen asked. "From what I've seen of him, he's got the kind of sly character that would do anything to get what he wants."

"What would he gain from killing Greg?"

"Piers was jealous of Greg's friendship with Alex," Helen said. "Didn't Eva say Greg and Alex grew up together? If they were close, Piers might have felt left out. He thought he wasn't getting his fair share of Alex's newfound wealth and fame. He figured the only way he could do that was to get rid of Greg."

"Piers seems super confident. He wouldn't be threatened by some computer geek." My phone signaled I had a message. It was from Zach.

I smiled. He was missing me and was sorry he hadn't been there to say goodbye. I typed a quick reply. I also missed him. But that was another problem to deal with. I had a pesky ghost hunt at home to solve. I still hadn't figured out what to do about the Amelia problem.

It was time for another cookie and then bed. Maybe in the morning, I'd figure a few of these ghost puzzles out.

It was after ten the next morning. I'd been waiting in the study for over an hour for Alex to appear. I'd wandered around the house to see if he was working in another room, but there'd been no sign of him.

Eva was also absent, as was Camilla, so I couldn't check with them to see if Alex had already left the house and forgotten to let me know.

My misgivings about this job increased the longer I waited.

Greg was also nowhere to be seen. After his fright last night when I'd revealed that Eva had liked him, he hadn't returned. Maybe I'd scared him off. Would that be such a bad thing? It would be nice not to have to worry about solving a ghost's problem, especially since I had one back home I should focus upon.

I stood and looked out the office window. Everything was quiet outside. Spring continued its battle with winter as a few fluffed-up sparrows hopped around on the grass.

I decided to do one more circuit downstairs to see if I could find Alex. He had to be somewhere. I had been tempted to go upstairs and try his bedroom, but if he was having a lie in, it would be rude to drag him out of his bed.

He was paying my salary, and so long as he kept doing that, I guess he could keep his own hours. It made me wonder what on earth I was doing here. If things didn't improve over the next few days, I would get in touch with the recruitment agency and see if they could find me something new.

Starting in the lounge, I decided to open the half-drawn curtains and let light in. Opening a window wouldn't be a bad idea either. The room smelled of cold baked beans and beer.

I walked over to the first window and yanked the curtain all the way back.

Something stirred behind me, and I jumped. On the couch lay Alex, a coat thrown over his head.

Flipper ran over and investigated Alex. He didn't move.

I took a step toward him and then stopped. Had he spent the night on the couch?

I looked over to see the wide-screen TV was still on and the computer game paused. Alex had probably been playing most of the night and had crashed out with exhaustion.

It couldn't do a person good to play computer games for that long. We would have to work on Alex's time management and put his priorities in order. He might run a successful business at the moment, but if he spent his days and nights playing computer games, it wouldn't last long.

The screen behind me bleeped. I turned and looked at it. There was a message sitting there.

Can we talk?

I stared at the screen and then looked back at Alex.

"Do you mean me?" I felt silly talking to a screen.

Yes. You. Are you alone?

I looked around the room. How could the computer hear what I'd just said? "No. Alex is asleep on the couch, and my dog is with me."

Then we can talk. A freaky image of an alien's elongated head appeared.

What did I have to say to an alien? "Okay. Let's talk."

"I'm Mickey Kill," a robotic sounding voice said.

"You can hear me?"

"I can. There's a web cam embedded into this screen, along with a mic."

Now, I really was getting freaked out. Could Mickey Kill see what was going on here the whole time? "How are things with you, Mickey?"

"Not great. Greg's dead."

"So I've been hearing," I said. "Did you know him?"

"He was a good guy. An amazing gamer. He even beat me a few times. He's a loss to the online community."

I checked Alex was still asleep before continuing. "His death was unusual."

"It was."

"Do you know anything about it?"

"I might."

"Would you like to share?"

"Can I trust you?"

"I should ask you the same thing," I said. "I'm talking to an image of an alien. You could be anybody."

"So could you."

"I'm sure a talented guy like you can check me out if you want to," I said. "I've got nothing to hide."

"I know. I've looked into your background."

I tried to hide my surprise. "What did you find?"

"You've had a lot of jobs."

He was right, but it wasn't out of choice that I had to leave so many of my previous jobs. Changes in circumstances with previous employers, not to mention the interference of ghosts, often led to me looking for new positions. "My work takes me to different places."

"And just before you leave, a murder gets solved."

I swallowed. Mickey Kill was scarily good at digging up information. "How odd."

"Were you involved in solving that gold heist?"

I opened my mouth, wondering whether to lie. "I have a friend who works in the police. He helped with that."

"More like you did," Mickey Kill said. "You help people in need. You help people who've had bad things done to them."

"Wouldn't anybody?" I asked. "If you knew someone was in trouble or had something bad done to them, you'd want to help."

"I guess so."

"So, why is it so odd that I do that?" If he started talking about me being able to see ghosts, I'd have a meltdown.

"I think you're... different."

"I'm the same as anyone," I said. "Nothing special."

Mickey Kill was silent for a moment. I wondered if he'd gone off-line. "I don't think Greg's death was an accident."

I took a deep breath. "What makes you say that?"

"He was a good guy but inexperienced. He let people take advantage of him. Greg wanted to change the world with his ideas. He had so many. He shared them with anyone who'd listen to him. That made him vulnerable."

"Do you think he shared his plans with the wrong person?" I asked.

"I do."

"What do you think that person did? Stole his plans?"

"That's exactly what happened," Mickey Kill said. "They didn't just take his plans; they claimed it was their idea so they could have all the money."

This was interesting. "Who would do that?"

"Why don't you check out the online app Alex made all his money on?" Mickey Kill said. "That's the reason Greg's dead."

Chapter 7

"Huh? What's happening? What's going on?" Alex rolled onto his side and fell off the couch.

I looked at the computer screen, still stunned by Mickey Kill's revelation. "Are you okay?"

Alex sat up abruptly and scrubbed a hand through his messy hair. "Sure. I'm fine. It happens all the time. I thought I heard talking."

"You must have dreamt it." I helped him to his feet. "Do you always sleep down here?"

"Some nights," Alex said. "I get distracted by the games. It's just easier to crash here than stumble upstairs. Besides, Mom doesn't like me waking her by making a noise if I go to bed late."

"What happened to Piers and Harriet?"

"I sent them home," Alex said. "Harriet can be a bit... distracting. I don't think she's really into her games. I need someone around who gets why I do this." He tucked his crumpled T-shirt into his jeans and then pulled it out again as if undecided as to which way looked better.

"I've been hearing about your friend Greg. He loved games as much as you do."

Alex stretched his arms in front of him and then rolled his shoulders. "Yeah, Greg loved his games. It was how we got to know each other. We set up the first computer game society at our school. Those computers were such a joke when I think about them. Hardly any memory and no color, but we loved playing games. We learned how to write basic code back then. Greg was always coming up with some new trick or coding sequence to make the games better."

I sat on the edge of the couch. "That sounds like fun."

"Most people would find it tedious," Alex said. "Are you sure you're not a secret gamer?"

"I used to play when I was a kid," I said. "Not so much now."

"You should," Alex said. "They're great. It's a good way to forget yourself and try living in a different world, with different rules and people. It's eye opening."

"It sounds it," I said. "I've been hearing about your online dating app. Did you design that with Greg?"

"Not really," Alex said. "I could murder a cup of tea. Tell you what, I'll open the dating app and you have a look through it while I go make some tea for us."

He surprised me. I'd expected him to ask me to make the tea. "Tea would be lovely."

"Give me a minute." Alex changed the view on the computer screen and opened the internet. He clicked on an image and a green screen appeared. "This is the basic layout of the app. You put your details in using the keyboard. I can guarantee you'll find your soulmate."

I laughed. "If only it was that easy."

"I promise you, it is. Spend a bit of time on the information you input. The algorithms will do the rest. Love isn't so tricky. Just make sure you're honest," Alex said as he walked to the door. "If you tell the computer you love long walks on the beach and cozy nights by the fire, when you actually like raving and eating fish and chips, you won't find your true life partner."

"I'll make sure I tell the truth." I grinned as I entered my details. Data couldn't be that accurate. Love had to be more than simply filling in a few boxes and letting a computer do the rest. Falling in love was about chemistry and romance, learning to deal with your partner's strange little quirks, such as having a dead wife haunting your house.

Ten minutes later, I'd filled out a dozen boxes. Alex returned with two mugs of tea and an enormous bowl of muesli.

He handed me my tea. "I hope you've already had breakfast. I didn't bring you anything to eat."

"I'm fine. I ate a while ago. So, what next?" I gestured at the screen.

"Hit the enter button and find your dream man."

I laughed again. "I already found him. You're going to be disappointed."

"Don't be so sure about that." Alex took a slurp of his tea as he settled on the couch next to me. "This app is ninety percent accurate. People just have to let go of a few hang-ups and embrace the magic of the system. It works."

I pressed the enter button and waited as the computer hunted for my Mr. Right. "Did you find Harriet on here?"

Alex grimaced. "She's not on here."

"How did you meet?"

"At a party, I think." Alex scrubbed his chin. "I can't remember. She's always just sort of been there. She'd turn up at the same places I went to, and we'd hang out. She likes to party. Harriet is always trying to drag me to the latest premier or the opening of some fancy new restaurant. That's not my thing. They never serve the sort of food I like and are full of people showing off their latest fashions or cars." He looked at his crumpled clothes.

"You must like her, though. She seems keen on you."

"Sure, she's nice enough." Alex's eyes brightened. "Look! Your results are in." He grabbed the keyboard and scrolled through the results. "Okay. So you like outdoorsy type of guys."

I smiled. "I do."

"You like guys who are practical and hands-on."

"Again, that's right."

"They must be an animal lover." Alex grinned and looked over to Lucy, who was asleep in the corner on a giant fluffy bed.

"That's an absolute definite."

"You've put here that they have to be single and can't have been married before." He raised his eyebrows. "Is them being married before a deal breaker?"

I gritted my teeth. Was it? I was trying hard to convince myself it wasn't. Zach's revelation about Amelia had really knocked me. "I guess I can handle it. So long as they are definitely divorced and the former wife is out of their life, preferably on another continent."

Alex nodded. "Fair enough. I've filled in any who are separated. No baggage required."

"Who does that leave me with?"

"These four guys." Alex brought up a picture of four men.

My eyes widened. It was like I was looking at pictures of Zach's brothers. I lowered my cup. "You have got to be kidding me."

"You don't like them?" Alex frowned and scrubbed a hand through his hair, making it stand on end. "Maybe there's something wrong with the data."

"No, it's not that." I read through the profile of the first guy. He loved nature and walks in the woods. He had two dogs and a house in the country. He also owned his own graphic design business and had a side-line in Japanese garden design.

"Is he your sort of thing?" Alex asked.

"Show me the next one." This dating app was good.

"This is hunky bachelor number two." Alex showed a picture of a dark-haired guy with stubble and piercing blue eyes. In his profile picture was a happy looking mongrel sitting next to him.

I groaned, not wanting to read about this one.

"Is he also no good?" Alex scrolled through the page. "It says here he owns a nature conservation business and spends his weekends camping. He owns a camper van and wants to run a rescue center for unwanted dogs when he retires."

"That sounds awful." Actually, it sounded like heaven.

"We could try hunky number three."

"No! I'm fine for hunks. I have all the hunk I need back home."

"If you didn't have a guy, would any of these fit your preference?"

"All of them sound too good to be true. How have you managed to be so accurate?"

Alex grinned and relaxed back in his seat. "I mine data from across the internet. I collate your history, searches, cookies, that sort of thing, run it through the dating algorithms, and we come out with your perfect partner."

"Is that even legal?"

"Sure. Do you remember seeing little messages about things called cookies when you look at websites?"

"I do. I ignore them."

"They don't ignore you. Everything you search for is remembered. For example, if you were looking for camping holidays, the cookies remember. If you like going on walks and were looking for a new route, that piece of data would be legally saved for me to come along and use it to find your Mr. Right."

"No wonder you made money on this app. It's incredible."

Alex's grin widened. "Thanks. I'm glad it's helping people find a soulmate."

"Has it helped you find love?"

Alex shook his head. "Not yet. I'm not ready for all that grown-up stuff. I'm too busy with the business. Speaking of which, I've been thinking about our working relationship."

"Do you have things you want me to help with?"

"Not as such. How about you take the rest of the week off?"

My eyebrows shot up. "That's nice of you. Don't you need me here?"

Alex shrugged. "You seem like a nice lady. I'm just not sure what to do with you."

I let out a gentle sigh. Alex calling me a lady made me feel about sixty. "You could let me take a look at the business admin. Didn't your mom say it needed pulling into shape?"

"The paper stuff is a mess. I scan everything, though. I have a copy of every piece of business paperwork I've ever received if the tax man comes asking questions."

"Even so, it can't hurt to have the paper copies neatly stored."

"That's boring."

"It's what you're paying me for."

"I'd feel guilty giving you something so dull to do. Like I said, take some time off; get to know the area. Maybe we can hang out together next week."

"Alexander Harold Hudson, don't you dare do that!" Camilla stood in the open doorway, her arms folded over her chest.

"Mom! I didn't know you were in." Alex spilled tea on his pants.

"I was in the garden. I overheard you trying to get rid of Lorna." Camilla walked into the room. "That will not happen. She's important. You must make good use of her."

"She doesn't want to do the filing," Alex said. "No one wants to file."

"I'm happy to file," I said. "In fact, I like it. It makes me happy bringing order to chaos."

"Then you'll be in seventh heaven when you see the mess of Alex's files. Plus, there are dozens of unanswered RSVPs to important events Alex is supposed to go to." Camilla stood in front of Alex. "I know you don't like the social scene, but there will be all sorts of opportunities you'll miss if you don't attend. Why not pick one event and go to that?"

Alex groaned and rubbed at the tea stain on his pants. "I'll think about it."

"More action less thinking," Camilla said. "It's time for you to rise above the rest and be the best. Start acting on improving yourself."

"I'm about to act," Alex said. "I've got a new level on my game to crack." His fingers inched toward the controller on the coffee table.

"Absolutely not!" Camilla snatched up the controller and tucked it under her arm.

"Mom! This is important."

"Not as important as keeping your business going. Ever since that incident with Greg, you haven't applied yourself."

Alex looked away. "You mean, ever since Greg was killed."

Camilla gave a dramatic sigh. "His death was a horrible accident. I understand you need time to mourn your friend. He wouldn't want to see you wasting your life like this. You always had such great ideas when you worked together."

"Maybe I need Greg to make the ideas happen." Alex stuffed an enormous spoonful of muesli into his mouth. Milk dripped on his T-shirt.

"You're fine on your own." Camilla gestured to the screen. "Not addressing the problems you have won't help."

"I don't have any problems," Alex said. "Neither do you. This is the house you wanted us to live in, so I got it for you."

"We all wanted this house," Camilla said. "It's a great location. You can make it into a family home when you're ready to settle down. Have you thought any more about finding a steady girlfriend?"

Alex's cheeks colored, and he shot me an apologetic look. "I'm working on it."

"Work harder." Camilla slapped the controller against her thigh. "You can't slack at every aspect of your life. Discipline, hard work, and focus, that's what you need. You must stop playing around."

Alex frowned. "I like playing around. I'm good at it. It's made me rich."

"Not anymore. You're the man of this house. You have to start acting like one. And you can begin by making use of Lorna. She's not here to make the place look pretty. She has a brain in her head, so make use of it."

I was sure there was a compliment somewhere in Camilla's words. "Shall I make a start with the RSVPs? I can gather them, sort them into the ones with the most business prospects, and you decide which to attend."

Alex twisted his mouth from side to side. "I guess we can do that."

"No guessing. You will do that." Camilla looked at me and shook her head. "Sometimes, I think my boy will never grow up." She turned and left the room, taking Alex's controller with her.

Alex finished his tea and slammed the mug down. "Sorry about that. Mom can be a bit..." he waved a hand in the air.

"She's only looking out for you. She wants to make sure you're happy." Alex was right, though, his mom was crazily sure of herself. I wouldn't want to get on the wrong side of her.

"I know. It still doesn't mean you have to sort through my messy paperwork. We can pretend you've done it, and I'll have a big bonfire at the weekend and burn it all. It can be our secret."

"No to the bonfire. I don't mind doing it." I looked at the computer screen. "What are you going to do about having no controller?"

Alex smiled and pulled an identical controller out from under the couch cushion. "It's always important to have a backup."

Chapter 8

I was surrounded by three huge stacks of paper as the afternoon light slid down the wall in the lounge. I could finally see an order to Alex's chaotic paperwork. I had a pile to shred, a pile to store, and a pile of queries.

"This is the final batch of invitations." I held up a stack of paper. So far, Alex had refused to go to any events. Some sounded amazing, from a new sushi restaurant in London where you selected the food using an app and a robot server came to your table, to a gaming conference in Las Vegas, showcasing developments in virtual reality immersive games.

"Tell them all thanks but no thanks." Alex paused his game. "I don't like crowds. Those things are always so hectic."

"What if I could find you an event that wasn't so noisy?"

"How about the opening of a new library? Or a silent disco?"

I smiled at him. Alex was a sweet guy. Naïve and a loner, but I liked him. "Those are both possibilities I've yet to find. I haven't finished looking, though."

"Let me know when you do. I might say yes."

"How about this one? It's a game launch in a water garden in Wiltshire."

"Nope. I don't like to travel."

"It's Wiltshire. It takes three hours in the car."

"That's too far. Besides, I get travel sick."

I sighed. "There's a games conference in London. That's not far from here."

"Where's it being held?"

"The O2 arena."

"That's way too big. Besides, I have a lousy sense of direction. I'd be lost for hours in that place and would miss the whole event."

"I can come with you."

Alex glanced at me. "Are you offering to hold my hand?"

I resisted the urge to roll my eyes. "I'm offering to come with you as your personal assistant and make sure you don't miss all the important bits. I'll arrange your travel and schedule. I can even sort out the food for the day. All you need to worry about is enjoying yourself and making the right contacts."

"Thanks. That's kind of you. I'm still not going."

"I'm not being kind. It's my job!" I checked through the next few invitations. Alex had important people wanting him at their events. Who knew the world of gaming had so many influential figures involved?

"Have you always avoided these kinds of events?" I asked.

Alex lowered his controller. "Not always. I never loved them. Greg used to think they were fun, though. He would talk to anyone who was interested in his latest game or app."

"You sound like you were a good team."

He nodded. "I liked having him around. I never felt like I had to make an effort when he was here. You know, I could just be me."

I got that. I was the same with Helen. She saw me at my worst and my best, and I knew she'd always want to be my best friend. "Maybe you could find a new Greg at one of these events."

Alex's nose wrinkled. He fixed his gaze on the screen. "There's no chance of that."

"Or you could take someone else. What about Harriet?"

Alex laughed. "At a games conference? She'd die of boredom, even if there was free champagne."

"Or Piers?"

He shook his head. "I'm not sure Piers would be into all of that. I don't know. He's fun to hang with sometimes..."

"But you're not sure why he's here?"

Alex shrugged. "I like the guy. He could be mean to Greg, though. He never outright bullied him, but they didn't get along. They were so different. Piers is a party guy. Greg liked the parties, but he didn't even drink. He went to chat with people, find a pretty girl to fall hopelessly in love with, or have a dance. He loved to dance, even though he had the rhythm of a squashed hedgehog."

"I suppose suggesting you take your mom to an event is out of the question?"

"That would be the height of un-coolness. I know I'm a gaming geek, but even I have my limits."

I shuffled through the pile of invitations. There must be some way I could get Alex out of this house.

"Are you bored enough to play yet?" Alex waved the controller in his hand.

"Trust me, you don't want me on your team. I'm hopeless at those kinds of games."

"Everyone is bad to start with. All you need to do is practice."

I shook my head. "No amount of practice will make me as good as you."

Alex laughed. "I am pretty good at this. I need to be. It's my business."

I stopped sorting through the invitations. "I thought apps were your thing?"

"Anything computer related interests me," Alex said. "The dating app made me the most money. But I love games. I've sold a few. I used to work on a flight simulator program as well. I made it as realistic as possible. You felt as if you were actually on a plane. It's used for training pilots."

"I wouldn't mind a go at that."

"No can do," Alex said. "I sold everything to a private contractor. When you make a sale like that, they take everything. It stops you from being tempted to sell the design again, with a few tweaks, to a competitor. The world of gaming, apps, and simulations is a murky place. Don't be fooled by my tea stained pants and messy hair. I'm working in a cutthroat industry."

I had to laugh. Alex couldn't look more harmless if he tried. Still, it made me wonder; could there be truth in his words? Was the gaming industry that ruthless? If it was, Greg could have gotten tangled up in something murky, and someone got rid of him. Maybe I needed to look at suspects on the other side of the computer screen.

My thoughts went to Mickey Kill. Could he be involved? He believed someone had killed Greg. What if he'd been deflecting suspicion from himself?

"How about this for a fun game?" Alex loaded a new game onto the screen. Bright sparks of green and pink shot across the screen, and unicorns danced in and out of view.

I placed the RSVPs down. "What's that?"

"I've had a few ideas for kids' games. I work on violent stuff and love the zombie kill games, but I don't want kids seeing that. It might mess with their heads. So, I've been working on a series of games involving unicorns."

I shuffled closer. "I'm listening. What do these unicorns do?"

"They're skilled. They keep the world safe from the evil Bog Globs who creep out from their lairs and suck the color from everything. Once your color has gone, you turn gray and die."

"What kind of things do these Bog Globs attack?" I reached toward the game controller. I could handle stopping an evil Bog Glob in its slimy tracks.

"Anything. They love people and animals. They'll suck the energy right out of them. As a Defender Unicorn, it's your job to defeat them."

"How?"

"The horn is an obvious weapon. You spear a Bog Glob with that. They have other abilities, too. There are glittery unicorn farts. And, have you ever had a unicorn belch in your face?"

I grinned. "Not recently."

"It's a thing of magical rainbow beauty. Bog Globs hate it." Alex returned my grin. "So, you want to play?"

I glanced at the piles of paperwork. "Five minutes won't hurt."

***

Three hours later, my wrists ached, my eyes burned, and my stomach hurt from where I'd laughed so much.

Alex's game was genius. The unicorns were hard core ninja fighters. Although the level of violence was not on a par with Alex's zombie game, it would still startle a few children.

I'd made it to level four and was desperate for a bathroom break but had to defeat three more Bog Globs attacking a pet rescue center.

"What's going on?" The icy cold tone of Harriet made us both jump.

"Harry, come in." Alex gestured her over. "I've been showing Lorna my new game. She's a natural on the controller. She killed five Bog Globs in her last attack."

"Don't call me Harry. You can see for yourself that I'm all woman." Harriet strode into the room and stared at the screen.

"Join us. See if you can beat Lorna. She's ace," Alex said.

I blushed at his praise. "This is beginner's luck. I'm still not sure what all the buttons on this controller do."

"You're great." Alex grinned at me.

"I'm sure she is." Harriet squashed herself between Alex and me, giving me a shove with her bony hip as she settled in.

Someone wasn't happy I was here. "I should call it a day. If I play anymore, I'll be dreaming about being attacked by a Bog Glob all night."

"No! Stay!" Alex said. "We're just getting going."

I handed the controller to him. "Another time. We've been playing for ages, and I still have to finish going through your RSVPs."

Harriet's sour face brightened. "What events are you going to, Alex? Don't forget about taking a plus one."

Alex glanced at Harriet. "I'm not going to any events."

"Oh, come on! We could do with a night out. A girl can only take so much zombie slasher nonsense before it gets boring."

"We can always play the unicorn game." Alex gestured at the screen and offered Harriet the controller.

She shoved it away. "Maybe you want to stay in and play with your much older... friend." Her gaze cut to me.

Older friend! I ignored her as I shuffled the papers into order.

"It's not that. You know I'm not into the glitzy stuff," Alex said.

"If Lesley went with you, I bet you'd go," Harriet said.

"Lesley?" Alex scratched his head. "Who's that?"

"I think Harriet means me." I gathered a stack of papers in my arms.

"Her name's Lorna," Alex said. "And *Lorna* gets that I don't want to go to some stuck-up place and play nice with people who want to stab me in the back."

"You're being paranoid. No one wants to do that." Harriet snaked an arm through Alex's. "We can go out and have fun."

"Was Greg being paranoid?" Alex muttered.

Harriet sat up straight. "What do you mean?"

"He knew people were interested in his apps and games."

"Of course they were. And they offered him a heap of money for them. There's nothing wrong with that."

I pretended to sort through the invitations in my hand as I listened to Harriet and Alex. Maybe my idea about a business rival getting tough with Greg hadn't been such a strange one.

"Greg had so much money, he didn't know what to do with it," Alex said.

"He could have spent it on me." Harriet giggled.

"He liked to spend it on good causes, not frilly dresses and expensive shoes." His gaze cut to Harriet.

"Oh! You're talking about his silly idea to give ten percent of his profits to charity." Harriet snuggled closer to Alex. "Greg was such a thoughtful guy, but giving away your money like that wasn't the smartest thing he'd ever come up with. I was glad it didn't happen."

"It was a great idea," Alex said. "I'll carry it on. From next month, I'm giving fifteen percent of all my profits to charity."

Harriet scowled at Alex. "What about our holiday?"

"You'll still get a holiday," Alex said. "The business makes plenty of money."

"Enough to take me to Antigua *and* Switzerland?"

Alex's fingers tightened on the controller. "If we have to. I was thinking of glamping, though."

"Yuck! Count me out if you're going to do something as ridiculous as that. Who wants to spend their holiday in some muddy old field in a tent with a few sparkles on it?"

"I do," Alex said. "You don't have to come. I wouldn't mind getting away and having some peace and quiet."

"Of course I'm going to come," Harriet said. "I wouldn't like to think of you all alone. You must rethink the glamping, though. The next time I'm in town, I'll grab some brochures for Antigua."

"I don't want to go there."

Harriet's hands clenched. "Maybe Lesley can do that for us?" She shot me a false looking smile and curled closer to Alex.

"It's Lorna." Alex pulled his arm free from Harriet. "She's not paid to do that. She's helping me with the business."

"I don't mind picking up brochures," I said. I definitely did, but wouldn't let the evil Harriet know she was getting to me.

"No! If Harriet wants to go to Antigua, she can research it herself," Alex said.

"You're so grumpy these days." Harriet pouted and ran a hand down Alex's arm. "Is there anything I can do to cheer you up?"

"Nothing I can think of," Alex said. "Unless you want to play a game with me."

Harriet's nose wrinkled. "I can play for a little while. So long as you promise to stop being such a grumpy pants."

"Lorna, why don't you play with us as well?" Alex asked. "You're getting really good."

"She's far too busy to get involved with our game." Harriet grabbed the game controller. "I'll play with you. Lorna can get on with her work."

I bit my tongue and smiled as serenely as possible. At least she was getting my name right. "Harriet's correct. I do need to get on."

"Finish that tomorrow," Alex said. "It's already getting late."

"Thanks. I'll just get this in order." I gathered the rest of the paperwork and headed out of the lounge. Having witnessed how possessive Harriet was of Alex, I could well imagine her resenting his friendship with Greg.

Perhaps Harriet thought Greg was stopping her from developing her relationship with Alex? It would be a good motive for wanting him out of the way. It also sounded like she hated Greg and Alex's idea of giving money to charity. It would have meant less for her to spend on expensive holidays. That was another reason to get rid of Greg.

The more I learnt of Greg, the more I liked him. He sounded like he'd been a smart guy with a conscience. Sadly, that conscience might have gotten him killed.

Chapter 9

After filing away the paperwork, I wandered to the kitchen with Flipper.

Helen stood by the stove, kneading dough so fiercely I figured it must have offended her.

"What are you making?" I grabbed an apple from the bowl in the center of the table and sat down.

"You won't believe what I'm about to tell you." Helen turned and frowned at me. "Alex sent me a text message this afternoon, saying he wanted to order takeout pizza for tonight."

"That's not a bad idea." It had been ages since I'd had a thin crust base loaded with pineapple and mushrooms.

"It's a hideous idea. I point-blank refused. I replied and told him there's no point in having me here if he isn't going to let me cook."

"Is that why you're punishing the bread?"

"It's not bread," Helen said. "I told him I'd make him the best pizza he's ever had. This is the base. Not that he deserves it."

"Your pizza will be amazing. Are we having pizza as well?" All I could think of was pineapple and mushrooms, all warm and gooey with cheese.

"I don't see why not." Helen returned to pounding the dough. "What toppings do you fancy?"

I grinned. "Guess."

"Gross pineapple and mushrooms. You're such a weirdo when it comes to pizza toppings."

"Those are excellent pizza toppings."

"Well, if you can find them in the fridge, you can eat them," Helen said. "The last time I looked, the fridge was sadly lacking both."

"I know! How about your famous sweet toppings pizza?"

Helen left the dough on the counter and sat at the table. "I haven't made a sweet pizza in ages. I could use fruit compote as a base, and we can add whatever we like on top. We can try cinnamon, chocolate, and banana."

"I'm sure I saw marshmallows in the cupboard," I said, warming up to the idea of this pizza. "Maybe we can try those."

"Marshmallow on pizza." Helen's eyes brightened. "I should be disgusted by that, but I'm not. Okay, let's have pizza tonight."

"And maybe a salad to offset all the junk we're about to eat."

"Naturally. Eat junk food with healthy food, and they cancel each other out. A salad will be no problem. I was going to make one for Alex, anyway, so I'll just make extra for us."

"He could do with eating more greens," I said. "He's paler than me."

"How was your first day working with Alex?" Helen jumped to her feet and got to work on the food, now humming happily under her breath. When it came to food, it didn't take much to cheer up Helen.

"Interesting. I like him. He talked about Greg today. He misses him."

"You're not thinking he's a suspect in Greg's death?"

"Not so much," I said. "Alex is just naïve. He's still young. He's been handed all this cash without being shown how to use it."

"Maybe you can help him spend his money."

"I don't think he needs any help with that," I said. "Harriet came in just as we were finishing up and was planning all kinds of expensive trips."

"Do you think she's after Alex's money?"

"I reckon so." I sliced my apple with a knife and ate a piece. It wasn't a patch on the sweet pizza we'd soon be enjoying. "Harriet was talking about wanting to book holidays abroad, expensive ones. She also mentioned Greg had a plan about giving some of the business profits to charity."

"Let me guess; she hated that?"

"Exactly right. Alex still wants to do it. She's not got complete control of him."

"Their relationship is odd," Helen said. "Alex doesn't even seem to like Harriet."

"I don't think he dislikes her. If she didn't come around, Alex wouldn't bother to see her. I think he lets her hang around him because it's easier than having an awkward conversation and telling her he's not interested."

"Do you think she had something to do with Greg's death?"

"It's possible. I wondered if she'd gotten jealous of their friendship and wanted Greg out of the way."

Helen grimaced. "There's nothing worse than a possessive girlfriend. It's important to keep tabs on your man, though. Speaking of which, I haven't heard from Gunner all day."

I grinned at her. "Maybe he's busy solving a big case."

"He always sends me at least one text message a day. I'm going to chase him up and see what he's up to." She wiped her hands, pulled her phone out, and sent him a message. "Has Greg been any help in narrowing down who's involved in his death?"

"He's not about," I said. "It's almost as if he's shy."

"Maybe he was like that when he was alive," Helen said. "Do ghosts carry personality traits over when they die?"

"I think so," I said. "I'm guessing he was a loner, like Alex."

"Or he could be off in ghost gaming heaven, playing some spectral mission." Helen grinned as she placed a bowl of salad on the table. "Eat the boring salad while I put the pizzas in the oven."

I quickly fed Flipper and then laid the table as I waited for the pizzas to cook. The enticing smell of melting marshmallows and chocolate filled the kitchen. My mouth watered.

Helen pulled out a large thin crust cheese and tomato pizza, which she sliced before plating. She added a hunk of homemade garlic bread and a side salad. "I'd better take this to his Lordship. He'd better appreciate it."

"It smells amazing." I was tempted to steal a piece of Alex's pizza as Helen passed me. "He'll love it."

As I waited for Helen to return, I grabbed my laptop and went online. Harriet wasn't the only suspect I was interested in.

"What are you looking at?" Helen asked as returned from the lounge. She hurried to the stove and removed our delicious smelling pizzas. It smelled like I was sitting in the middle of a candy store.

"Piers Torrington," I said. "I took an instant dislike to the guy when we met."

"Any man who corners a woman against the kitchen counter isn't a nice guy," Helen said as she sliced up the pizzas and sat down. "He was so sure of himself. He thought I should be grateful for his unwanted attentions."

"Not only that, but he disliked Greg," I said. "He had nothing good to say about him."

"Piers hated Greg enough to kill him?" Helen grabbed the largest piece of pizza and took a bite. She let out a groan of pleasure.

I looked up to see chocolate on her chin and a smile on her face.

"Try this. The marshmallows and chocolate combination is amazing," she said.

I grabbed a slice. It tasted fantastic. I forgot all about the dreadful Piers for a moment. The base was slightly sweet. The fruit compote had soaked into it, giving it a strawberry tang. It was the marshmallow and chocolate combination that made it. "We'll have to make this a regular thing."

"Agreed," Helen said. "So, Piers? What have you found out about him?"

I scrolled through my search results. "There are lots of images of him in London, flashing his money around."

"Where does he work?"

"I can't find any information about him having a job. His parents are wealthy. They run a property development company."

"I bet Piers lives off their income," Helen said. "He's too lazy to get his own job but is happy to sponge off others."

"Harriet said he was an entrepreneur but didn't say what he did. Eva mentioned he benefited from the family income."

"He's a professional sponger *and* a sleaze."

"It could be he's sponging off Alex," I said. "Maybe Piers figured he was onto a good thing and didn't want Greg around to notice what he was up to."

"Greg could have noticed," Helen said. "If Piers realized Greg was getting suspicious of his friendship with Alex, he'd have needed him out of the way before he told Alex what was going on. Maybe Piers was stealing from Alex and Greg found out. That would be an excellent motive to kill him."

I clicked a search result. "There's a picture of Piers and his parents standing outside the family home."

"I bet they live in an enormous house," Helen said. "I doubt Piers does understated."

"It is pretty big." I looked at the large detached cottage with a thatched roof. "It's only in the next village."

"We should head over there. We can ask the neighbors and see what they think of Piers."

"We have to start somewhere. Piers is as good a suspect as Harriet." I finished my first slice of pizza and set to work on the second.

"I could make the pizza to go," Helen said.

I looked at the sticky marshmallow and chocolate mess on my fingers. "Best we eat it here. You'll only crash the car because you're too focused on stuffing your face with pizza."

"I've never crashed in my life. And I never stuff my face with anything."

I looked at the smears of chocolate around Helen's mouth. "You keep telling yourself that."

Half an hour later, we were in Helen's car, heading toward the neighboring village, St. Clements Mount. Flipper was in his usual place on the backseat.

We coasted downhill, the lanes getting increasingly narrow as we entered the village.

"Do you know where Piers's house is?" Helen asked as we reached a crossroad.

"It won't be hard to find," I said. "This place is tiny, and the house is huge. It's set back off the road behind a white fence and has conifers at the entrance."

"I'll do a circuit of the village and see if we can find it," Helen said.

I kept a look out for the house as Helen drove. The village was beautiful. The front gardens were immaculately tended. There was a sign on the village green, saying: *winner of the best kept village*. It looked like the residents took a lot of pride in where they lived.

We passed a duck pond and a cute looking pub with a wonky sign out the front.

"Any sign of the house?" Helen asked.

"It must be off the main road," I said. "Let's look down the side roads."

We tried the first road without success, but had luck as we turned the corner.

"That's it," I said, bringing up a picture of the house on my phone. "I'm sure of it."

Helen stopped the car. We sat looking at the house for a moment.

"There are no neighbors to talk to," Helen said. "This looks like the only house on the lane."

I climbed out, Helen and Flipper following me. The evening was quiet. There was no traffic noise or people around. It was a lovely, peaceful setting.

"You're not thinking about going to the house, are you?" Helen asked.

"If Piers spots us, you can tell him you've changed your mind and want a life of adventure and excitement wrapped in his arms." I smiled at her. "I'll sneak around the back and have a look inside, while you keep him busy."

"Don't be gross." Helen scowled at me. "I wouldn't date Piers for all the chocolate cake in the world."

I tilted my head. "Can you hear a squeaking sound?"

Helen looked around. "I hear something. A squealing noise. Maybe Piers has fallen down a hole and needs help. Before you ask, I'm not helping him."

"It sounds like a pig, not a person. And not a happy pig." I crossed the lane and stared through a gap in the fence. "It's coming from the other side of this fence."

"Could be there's a farm around here," Helen said. "It's rural enough."

Flipper nudged my leg with his nose and stared at the fence.

"Flipper's sensing something's off." I hated to hear an animal in distress. I walked to the end of the fence. "Maybe we should take a look."

"What if Piers spots us?"

"We'll sneak in and out," I said. "No one will see us. I need to make sure the pig's okay."

"I have a bad feeling about this." Helen followed me to the gate.

I tried the latch, and it opened silently. "You see, there's no trouble getting in. I bet they don't even lock their back doors. It's so safe around here. We'll take a quick look and then leave. We can stop in at the pub and ask about Piers when we're done here."

"Actually, I wouldn't mind a shandy," Helen said. "But make this quick. I don't want to get arrested for breaking and entering."

"We're not going anywhere near the house." I could still hear the pig. Accompanying it was the faint roar of an engine. "If anyone finds us, we can say we got lost and were looking for directions."

Helen grabbed hold of the back of my jacket as we snuck past the trees, skirting the edge of the garden. There was a light on in the ground floor of the house, but I couldn't see anyone inside.

"What's that roaring noise?" Helen whispered.

"The engine, you mean?"

"Yes. It sounds like a tractor."

"It sounds more like a bike," I said.

We reached the edge of the trees and ran around the side of the house until we got to the back garden. The sound of the engine and the pig squeals grew louder.

Flipper suddenly ran out of the shadows and raced through the garden.

"Come back!" I whispered loudly.

Flipper ignored me and kept running.

"He'll reveal us if he's not careful," Helen said.

"He's worried about the pig," I said. "Come on. We need to see what's going on."

I ran after Flipper, and Helen followed me. At least now, I had a good reason for being there. I could say my badly-behaved dog had slipped his leash and run off. It was close to the truth.

Racing past a high box hedge and around the corner, I saw a field surrounded by wooden fencing. In the field was a single pig running around and squealing. My pulse raced. The poor pig was being chased by someone on a quad bike.

I spotted Flipper running toward the pig. "Stop! Come back!" I jumped over the wooden fence and chased after him.

The pig changed direction to avoid the idiot chasing it on the quad bike. It ran straight at me.

It wasn't a big pig. In fact, it looked similar to Alex's pet pig, Lucy. But the pig was running fast, and if it hit me, I'd go flying.

I swiftly changed direction. The pig avoided me, racing back toward its sty.

The person on the quad bike slowed. He removed his helmet. It was Piers!

"What are you doing here?" He looked at me and frowned as he ran his hand through his hair.

"I came to find out what was wrong with the pig," I said. "Why are you chasing it?"

Piers shrugged. "She needs exercising."

"You're scaring her."

"Pigs don't get scared," Piers said. "They're too stupid for that. It's just a bit of fun."

"Of course they get scared." I scowled at Piers. "She's not stupid. Pigs are very intelligent. She's almost as intelligent as Flipper."

Piers frowned. "Who's Flipper?"

"My dog." I gestured to Flipper, who was on alert, his attention fixed to Piers.

"There's nothing intelligent about that beast either," Piers said.

"What's going on?" Helen hurried up behind me.

"Piers is being cruel. He thinks it's okay to scare this pig." I glared at him. "Pigs and dogs have the same intellect as a three-year-old child."

"Which hardly makes them Einstein."

"Do you even know who Einstein is?" Helen asked.

Piers frowned. "Some geek who invented the theory of electricity."

"Was someone saying something about a lack of genius around here?" Helen raised her eyebrows at me.

"Whatever." Piers shrugged. "I don't care about your ugly dog."

"Don't listen to him, Flipper. Everyone knows you're beautiful," Helen said.

Piers snorted a laugh. "You're as sad as Alex, talking to your pet."

"I thought Alex was your friend," I said.

Piers glared at me. "Who I'm friends with is none of your business. Now, get off my land. You're not welcome."

"I'm not leaving until you stop chasing that pig," I said.

Piers rolled the quad bike closer and revved the engine. "It's time for you to go. Take your mangy dog, as well, before I run him over."

"Don't you dare." I grabbed hold of Flipper and kept him close to my side. "And leave that pig alone."

Piers rolled the quad bike even nearer.

I stepped backward rapidly, closer to the pig's enclosure. I could hear her concerned sounding grunts.

"If you don't leave, I'll call the police and have you arrested," Piers snarled.

"Do that," I said. "I'll tell them how you're mistreating this pig. There are laws against animal cruelty."

"She's my pig," Piers said. "I can do what I like with her. Maybe next week, I'll make her into bacon sandwiches."

"Don't be disgusting," Helen said. "She's a family pet."

"She's a stupid animal," Piers said. "And she's mine, so I get to do what I like with her. It's the same with all women."

"Did you seriously just compare your relationship with this pig to having a girlfriend?" I asked.

"No wonder he's single," Helen said.

Piers's cheeks flushed a deep crimson. "She's the same as a stupid girlfriend. She gets under your feet, she makes too much noise and mess, and she's expensive to feed."

We backed up as Piers revved the engine again.

"I can have any woman I want, you included," he said.

"You won't get anything by threatening us," I said. "Now, back off and leave the pig alone."

Piers climbed off the quad bike and stalked toward us. "Make me."

I hit the side of the pig's enclosure with the back of my thighs and glared up at Piers as he invaded my personal space. Behind me, the pig snorted.

"Maybe we should speak to your parents," Helen said. "Aren't you still living at home? None of this is yours, is it?"

"It will be." Piers flashed a glare at Helen. "Anyway, what do you know about it? Have you changed your mind about my offer for some fun, now you see how rich I am?"

"Nothing you can do or say will convince me to change my mind about you," Helen said.

Piers shrugged again. "Like I said, your loss." He shoved me on the shoulder. "Leave. Now."

Flipper growled and bared his teeth at Piers.

"It's okay." I petted Flipper's head. "This young man won't do us any harm. In fact, he's going to back off, let us take his pig, and then we'll leave."

"You're not taking my pig," Piers said.

"You're not looking after her," I said. "She was terrified. I could hear her distressed squealing from the road."

"That's still none of your business," Piers said.

"Animal cruelty is always my business."

"I bet your parents won't be impressed when they find out what you're doing," Helen said. "I expect they think you're out looking for a job and hoping you'll move out soon, not chasing some poor animal around a field for entertainment."

"Don't you dare get my parents involved in this," Worry flashed across Piers's face. "Helen's right," I said. "They need to know what you're doing. Then maybe they'll kick you out. Imagine that. You'll have to earn your own money."

Piers scowled. "Exactly who are you? How do you know anything about me?"

"I know enough not to trust you," I said. "We're going to leave and take the pig with us."

"No chance." Piers walked to the front of the sty and stepped inside, folding his arms over his chest and barricading the way in. "You'll have to go through me first."

I glanced at Helen. Neither of us was built for fighting. I was still determined to get that pig out. "Maybe we should call the police."

Piers smirked. "My uncle is the local sergeant. He'll be more interested in you trespassing on private property than what I'm doing with a sausage on legs."

That was my bluff gone badly wrong. "Helen, go over to the house and ask to speak to Piers's parents."

"You stay right where you are." Piers lunged at Helen, but she skipped out of his way.

Flipper growled and took a menacing step toward Piers.

"Keep your dog under control," Piers said. "I'm happy to have it shot if it bites me."

"He'll only bite you if you keep threatening Helen and me," I said. "Hand over the pig, and we'll leave you alone."

"That's not going to happen."

I noticed the pig had come closer when we'd been talking. She was looking at Flipper, her gaze interested as if she thought she might have found a friend. She was so close I could almost grab her. "Fine. Then we'll leave."

"What about the pig?" Helen gestured to the sty. "We can't leave her here. He's going to make her into bacon sandwiches."

"Piers won't do that," I said. "Who will he have to play with if his pig is gone?"

"You know nothing about me," Piers spat. "I have plenty of friends. Get out of here before I do have you arrested. I'm not messing around this time."

"Neither am I." I turned and walked away, Flipper by my side, and Helen hurrying along next to me.

"What are you doing?" Helen tugged my sleeve. "I can't believe you're leaving that pig behind."

"I'm not." I slowed and turned. I'd been teaching Flipper a few tricks, and he knew the perfect trick to help us out and set the pig free.

Helen stopped walking. "You're up to something."

I gestured at Flipper and then pointed at Piers. "Jump."

Flipper's ears pricked up. He raced back to the pig sty. He launched himself at Piers, just as the pig lined herself up so Piers tripped over her and fell into the muck, Flipper landing on top of him.

Helen laughed. "That's genius! And Piers thought they were stupid. Well done, Flipper and pig."

I watched with delight as the pig and Flipper touched noses then turned and ran together across the field toward us.

"That's it, you two. Let's get out of here." I suppressed a laugh as Piers rolled around in the mud. He deserved nothing less.

Flipper and the pig reached us. I petted Flipper on the head. "That was perfect, you clever dog. You'll get a big treat when we get back to the house."

I looked at the pig. She was panting and had several sores on her body. My loathing for Piers grew. He'd not been looking after this animal for some time. She wasn't large, so I scooped her into my arms, and we ran back to the car.

"Wait! You can't steal my pig," Piers yelled.

I glanced over my shoulder to see him on his knees. "Keep going," I said to Helen.

"What are you going to do with the pig?" she asked.

"She's coming back to the house with us."

"You want to put her in the car?"

"I'm hardly going to walk back with her in my arms."

"Then you're paying for having it cleaned when her trotters get mud everywhere," Helen said.

"You wouldn't abandon this pig for the sake of a little mud, would you?"

Helen looked at the pig and sighed. "She is kind of cute. But she's still covered in mud."

"I'll sit with her in the back seat on my lap. I'm happy to get covered in mud so long as we get her out of here."

"And away from the hideous Piers," Helen said. "How are we going to explain having Piers's pig, though?"

"We'll think of something." I let Helen open the back seat of her car for me and slid in, keeping the pig on my lap. She seemed remarkably calm, given we were abducting her. Maybe she was relieved to be away from Piers and his cruelty.

Flipper hopped in alongside me and gave the pig a thorough sniff before lying down next to us. He didn't seem disappointed in having another new friend of the pig variety.

"Get us out of here," I said to Helen. "We don't need Piers calling his uncle and having us arrested for pig rustling."

"He might still do that. At least we've rescued the pig. Anyone who sees the state she's in will be on our side." Helen roared the engine, wheel spun the car around, and shot us away from the scene of the crime.

Chapter 10

We'd been sitting in Helen's car for ten minutes, trying to figure out what to do with our stolen pig.

"We can't have the pig in the house," I said. "Alex has Lucy around, but she's house-trained. Seeing the state of this little one's enclosure, I don't think that's the case with her."

"We can hide her in an outbuilding," Helen said. "There are several around the back."

"That could work if we can find one that's secure and make sure she's got something soft to sleep on and food and water. We can keep her there for a few days until we figure out a long-term solution."

"Well, we can't stay in here, and neither can the pig," Helen said. "As cute as she is, she sort of stinks."

Helen was right. I now smelled of an unhealthy mix of damp straw, pig muck, and mud. "Let's see if we can find somewhere to put her."

We all climbed out of the car. I kept hold of the pig, not wanting her to run off and get lost. We crept around the side of the house and over to the outbuildings.

We were just checking the first one, when an overhead light blinked on, dazzling us. Before we had a chance to hide, the back door opened.

"Lorna! And Helen! When the security light went off, I thought someone was trying to break in." Camilla stood on the back doorstep, dressed in a cream robe. She looked ready for bed.

"Sorry to disturb you," I said, standing there with the pig in my arms. There was nothing we could do. We'd been caught with a stolen pig in hand.

"What are you doing out here at night?" Her gaze went to the pig. "And you have a muddy friend."

"We're looking after her," Helen said swiftly. "For Piers."

"That's Piers's pig?" Camilla took a step forward. "I thought she looked familiar. I haven't seen her since she was tiny. What's he doing lending you his pig?"

"He asked us to look after her. He said he wasn't going to be around much for a while." I thought my lie sounded convincing.

"And Piers's pig will be good company for Lucy," Helen said.

I nodded. "Pigs are sociable animals. They like to have other pigs around."

Camilla gave us a bemused smile. "I didn't realize you and Piers were such good friends."

"We're not," I said. "Not really. But I love animals and didn't like to think of this pig all alone."

"I hope you don't mind," Helen said. "We were looking for somewhere to put her for the night."

"You're in the right place," Camilla said. "Most of these buildings have equipment in them. Lucy sometimes goes in the one at the end when she fancies slumming it and not sleeping in the house. You can put your pig in there for the night."

"Thanks. Sorry again for disturbing you," I said. "I thought it was a bit late to come in and ask for a bed for the pig."

"That's no problem," Camilla said. "I was making myself a cup of cocoa before turning in."

"That sounds like a good idea," Helen said. "Perhaps we can have cocoa as well."

"Let's deal with this pig first," I whispered.

"How have things been going with Alex, today?" Camilla stepped closer. "I know he can be a little tricky to work with. I'm sure you'll sort him out."

"Things have been going great." I omitted the fact I'd played a computer game with Alex for hours. Camilla wouldn't approve.

"That's good," Camilla said. "All he needs is a firm hand. Discipline never hurt anybody. I spent the longest time trying to convince him to join the Army. That would have sorted him out. He'd have a routine, a hierarchy to respect, and a job for life. But he wasn't keen."

I raised my eyebrows. I couldn't imagine anyone less likely to join the Army than Alex. "We'll get it all sorted. A few more days on the paperwork and I'll have everything up-to-date."

"That sounds excellent," Camilla said. "Make sure you girls aren't up for much longer. We all have busy days tomorrow."

"We'll be right in." I hurried to the end outbuilding and placed the pig inside. There was already a trough with food for Lucy and a bowl of water.

"Sort out that straw," I said to Helen as I stroked the pig and made sure she was calm.

"I'm not getting mucky," Helen said. "You're already covered in mud. You deal with the pig's bed."

She had a point. "Fine. You go get some warm water so I can clean the sores on the pig and see if we can get her comfortable." I kicked the straw into what looked like a comfortable pile as I waited for Helen to return. It was the perfect overnight retreat for a pig who needed somewhere to chill out after a horrible ordeal.

When I turned around, the pig was already eating. Flipper sat next to her, a curious look on his face. Maybe he was trying to figure out whether he wanted another pig friend or not.

"You need to get changed." Helen looked down at my mud-spattered clothes as she returned with a bowl of water and a clean sponge.

"I don't mind a bit of mud." I knelt next to the pig and gently stroked her head. She flinched away the first couple of times, but then relaxed and continued eating. "You're safe here with us. You get some rest, and we'll come and see you in the morning." I washed her sores and made sure they were clean of mud.

I followed Helen out of the outhouse and locked the door.

"Piers will be spitting mad after what we've done," Helen said. "He was wearing designer clothes when he landed in all that muck."

"Then he's an even bigger idiot for wearing expensive clothes when riding a quad bike," I said. "From the way he was treating the pig, he doesn't want her. When he's calmed down and had a shower, he'll see this is for the best."

"I hope so," Helen said. "I thought he was going to run us over with his quad bike."

"I get the impression Piers is used to getting his own way. He doesn't like it when people stand up to him," I said. "We'd better watch our backs, just in case he gets mean."

Helen was making us hot cocoa while I washed my hands, when the back door was shoved open and Piers stalked in. He'd changed out of his mud-covered clothes but still had the slight odor of pig sty about him.

"Where is she?" he demanded.

I pushed back my shoulders and glared at him. "I don't know who you're talking about."

Piers's eyes narrowed. "What have you done with Priscilla?"

"That's the name of your pig?"

"I didn't name her," he growled. "Alex named the dumb pigs."

"Well, Priscilla is safely out of your reach. You're not getting her back," I said.

"She's mine!"

"Not anymore," I said. "I'll take good care of her and make sure no one torments her ever again. You're not fit to look after an animal."

"Lorna's right," Helen said, coming to stand beside me. "You should be ashamed of yourself."

"I'm ashamed of nothing," Piers said. "And I don't appreciate it when people steal from me."

I stepped closer to Piers and lowered my voice. "You will not do anything about this. If you do, I'll reveal your cruelty to Alex. He's not going to think much of you once he realizes what a nasty piece of work you really are."

"You wouldn't dare. He'd never believe you."

"I think he would. I'm getting on well with Alex. I'm sure he'll be interested in what I have to say. And when I show him the condition Priscilla is in, he'll know you've not been looking after her properly. Sores like that don't develop on a pig's skin overnight. He'll kick you out of his exclusive club. Then where will you be?"

"Alex trusts me," Piers said. "I'll say the pig got the injuries by accident."

"He owns a pig," I said. "He'll know injuries like that aren't accidental. He won't want you around when he sees what you've done to Priscilla."

"So, back off," Helen said. "Priscilla lives with us now. You'll tell Alex that you gave her to us as a gift."

Piers scowled. "I'd never give either of you anything."

"I can well believe that." Piers was clearly the taker in every relationship. "This time, you're making an exception. You like me and Helen so much that you gave us your prize pig. That'll make you look good in Alex's eyes."

"That wretched pig is nothing but trouble, anyway." Piers stalked to the kitchen door. "Not a word to Alex. I'll tell him I gave the stupid pig to you. You make sure that's what he thinks. If you tell him otherwise, I'll make sure you both lose your jobs."

I didn't think Piers would do that, but I was happy to play along if we got to keep Priscilla safe and out of his sick little hands. "It's a deal."

Piers yanked open the door and slammed it shut behind him.

"If we didn't have a number one suspect in Greg's death, we do now." I glanced at the door leading into the garden. "You don't think he'll take Priscilla?"

"No. The door lock is strong. She's safe here with us. And you're right. He's our top suspect. He must have been the one who shot Greg. There's not a good bone in his nasty little body. He's selfish, he only thinks about himself, and he uses people."

"How can we prove that?" I asked. "So far, all we know for sure is that he's a nasty piece of work who enjoys torturing animals."

"That's a good start," Helen said. "Don't most serial killers start by torturing animals?"

"The police will need more to go on than that," I said. "We need to do more digging into Piers's background, and see what dirty little secrets he's hiding."

"We can follow him," Helen said. "See if he goes to any seedy gambling dens and blows a ton of money. Or has a secret girlfriend with expensive tastes he needs to fund."

"I'll start with doing more research online before we tail him," I said. "We already know he likes the high life. Maybe there's more we can find out without risking getting run over by his quad bike." I tensed as the kitchen door swung open, expecting to see Piers back for a re-match.

Eva strode into the kitchen, wearing a floor-length black dress and matching eyeshadow. "What have you done to Piers? I've never seen him so angry."

"What makes you think we had anything to do with that?" I asked.

"Because he came stomping away from the kitchen and into the lounge," Eva said. She looked down at the floor. "And, well, I may have... heard you arguing."

"That was nothing." Had Eva been listening in?

"It sounded like something to me," Eva said. "I'm glad you're not friends with him. Piers is not a nice guy."

"We figured that out for ourselves," Helen said. "What's he done to you to make you dislike him so much?"

"Nothing in particular." Eva plucked at the sleeve of her dress. "He's just generally horrible to anyone he doesn't think can give him what he wants."

"Would that include Greg?" I asked.

"He was always so horrible to Gregory," Eva said. "I don't know why he put up with it. But Gregory was such a nice guy, he could never stay angry with anyone for long."

"Did you ever see them arguing?" I asked.

"Piers mainly put Gregory down or made fun of him," Eva said. "It was always subtle. If I ever called him out over it, he'd deny it. He always pretended it was a joke. I knew he was being serious, though."

That was another black mark against Piers's name. "We're definitely not in the Piers Torrington fan club," I said. "I'm not sure he's a good friend to your brother."

"Then that's Alex's fault for letting Piers hang around here all the time. My brother can be a knucklehead. So long as he gets someone to play on his dumb game, that's all he cares about."

"Alex needs better friends, especially now Greg has gone."

"He's got Harriet." Eva raised her eyebrows and grinned.

"She's the perfect girlfriend." I returned Eva's grin.

"You know, if you want to get one up on Piers, I've got the perfect way to do that." Eva smiled evilly.

"We're not out for any revenge," I said.

"Priscilla needs justice, though," Helen said.

"Priscilla? Piers's pig? What's she got to do with this?" Eva stared at Helen.

"Nothing at all." I shot Helen a warning look. "We're simply looking after Priscilla from now on. Piers is too busy to take care of her."

Eva shrugged. "I never thought he liked that pig. He only bought them so he could have something in common with Alex. Alex adores Lucy and was delighted when Piers arrived with the piglets. Piers never mentions Priscilla. I wondered if she was even still around."

"She's definitely around," I said. "She's staying here."

"Lucy will love that," Eva said. "Now, about getting even with Piers. I promise you no one will get hurt. Well, the only thing that will get hurt is Piers's ego. That always needs deflating."

I had to admit I was intrigued by Eva's offer. "What do we need to do?"

"Follow me," Eva said. "We need to go to my room."

We hurried up the stairs and into Eva's bedroom. It was a surprising contrast to her ever-present black clothing. There was a large double bed covered in a cream throw and a dozen fluffy pillows. There were several teddy bears squashed among the pillows. A sheer pink fabric covered the window, and her dressing table was covered in sparkling fairy lights. Set up in the corner of the room was a huge flat screen TV and a low seat.

"This is where I play my computer games," Eva said. "When I've had enough of dealing with Harriet and Piers, I come up here and play on my own."

"It's a nice room. But how is this going to help us get back at Piers?" Helen asked.

"You need to play against him in a game." Eva gestured to the screen.

Helen laughed. "You want us to fight Piers online?"

Eva grinned at us. "He thinks he's the best gamer around, despite the fact I've beaten him loads of times."

"He must hate that," I said.

"He has no idea it's me," Eva said. "I sign into all games under a pseudonym. I call myself the Hellion. Piers is always going on about the rivalry he has with the Hellion. He'd die of shame if he knew it was a girl beating him."

"I don't play computer games," Helen said. "I'll be no help to you. How about you, Lorna?"

"I know the basics," I said. "But I could never go up against an experienced gamer and expect to win."

"That's where this comes in." Eva pulled out a sheet of paper from beside the TV screen. "It's a cheat sheet. There's always a workaround for the most complicated things in games. We can beat him and teach him a lesson."

"I don't mind cheating if it's for a good cause," Helen said. "Do you think we can really do this?"

I did like the idea. We could get back at Piers for being so awful to Priscilla without him even knowing it.

"What do you think?" Eva asked. "Do you fancy a game?"

I took the controller she held out. "Why not? Let's play with Piers and teach him a lesson."

Chapter 11

We spent the next twenty minutes running through the basics of the game. It was an alien attack game. You joined as a squad of battle-hardened warriors and fought against the evil alien enemy who'd arrived on Earth with plans to decimate the planet. It was suitably gruesome and violent, just the sort of thing I imagined Piers would love.

Once I'd gotten the hang of the controller and how to shoot, it seemed simple enough.

Helen, on the other hand, was not so adept with her controller.

"Why doesn't it do what I want it to do?" She bashed one of the keys.

"What do you want to do?" Eva asked.

"Shoot that alien." Helen gestured at the screen. "The one with the fangs that's charging at me."

"Hit the fire button," Eva said, her tone sounding like she was talking to a five-year-old. "It's the yellow one."

"Oh! I thought it was the red one." Helen pressed the button and squeaked. "I killed the alien."

"Well done," Eva said dryly. "Okay, are you both ready? We'll go in as a squad of three, fighting in the same group as Piers. When his back is turned, we'll start shooting."

"How do you know he'll want to play with us?" I asked.

"He never turns down a gaming invitation from me," Eva said. "He's always looking to get his own revenge on my character. Piers wants to be the squad member who gets the most alien kills, even if that means leaving his team members behind."

"Does he play dirty?"

"I can guarantee it," Eva said. "He's no match for me. Piers has the attention span of a gnat. Distract him with a few aliens and explosions, and he won't see us coming."

"What's our squad name going to be?" Helen asked.

"I was going to keep it simple and call us the Hellion squad," Eva said.

"That's too violent," Helen said. "How about the Awesome Chicks' squad?"

Eva's eyebrows quirked. "This is an alien attack game. You don't get many awesome chicks playing."

"I bet there are a few," I said. "But maybe that's not the best name."

"The Feisty Ladies gang," Helen said. "That has a nice ring to it. Or we could be the Belle Ball Busters."

"That's not so terrible," Eva said.

"We should stick to the Hellion squad," I said. "At least then, Piers will know who he's dealing with."

"Agreed," Eva said. "Let's issue the invitation and get started on humiliating Piers."

I felt surprisingly tense that we were about to go up against Piers in a shoot 'em up game. Of course, it wasn't real, but I really wanted to get my own back on such an unpleasant person.

I studied the character I'd chosen for the game. He was an enormous, muscled guy, with a crewcut and scars on his face. He carried an automatic weapon and a flamethrower. He looked more than capable of taking down Piers.

"We're in." Eva flashed us both a smile. "Now, remember, we're playing alongside Piers to start. We're supposed to be on the same side. Our target is Thunder Mountain. Whichever squad gets there first gets the bonus."

"You mean we can't blow Piers's character's head off straightaway?" Helen's bottom lip jutted out.

"You'll be able to kill him eventually," Eva said. "We need to draw him in first and make him think we're on his side. Once he gets distracted by upping the number of alien kills he's made, then we can turn on him."

Seeing the evil glint in Eva's eyes, it reminded me she was also on my suspect list for Greg's death. She certainly had a vengeful streak in her, even though she was enacting that vengeance through a computer game.

"Follow me and try to keep up," Eva said as the game started, and we entered a dark, creepy looking cave.

Helen squealed and hit the fire button as a small alien with glowing eyes dropped from the ceiling in front of her.

"Nice shooting," I said.

"I'm getting good at this," Helen said.

"That one would have done nothing more than chew on your arm," Eva said. "It's the ten-foot aliens that spit acid you need to be careful of."

Helen grimaced. "I'll watch out for those."

A message flashed onto the screen. *Are you ready to die, Hellion?*

Eva smiled. "That's Piers being his usual charming self."

I stared at the screen name he used. "He calls himself King Stud?"

"King Idiot, more like," Helen muttered.

"He's so pathetic," Eva said. "We'll show everyone else in this game he's anything but a king." She typed back a quick message. *Never going to happen, loser.*

You've been lucky so far, Piers replied. *When you're taken down, I'll be there to watch and finish you off.*

"He's such a sweet talker," I said.

Eva shrugged. "This is his true personality you're seeing. He makes out it's an act and he's playing the big man. If he could be like this in the real world and get away with it, I know he would. He'll stop at nothing to get what he wants."

I glanced at Helen, and she gave me a knowing nod. That could have been what happened with Greg. Piers wanted him gone, so he made it happen.

"Oh my goodness," Helen squeaked. "What on earth is that?"

"I'll get it." I fired at the enormous alien as it charged toward us.

"This one needs a joint effort," Eva said. "Keep firing both of you. I'll keep an eye on Piers. He's sneaky enough to attack us while we're protecting ourselves."

"I can't get this controller to work!" Helen kept hitting the wrong key.

"Hit the fire button," I said as the alien grew nearer. "The yellow one!"

"I am hitting the fire button."

"No! You're running straight into the jaws of the alien."

Helen kept pressing the same button. The alien grabbed her and bit her character in two.

She gasped. "That's not supposed to happen! I've got another life, haven't I?"

Eva grimaced and shook her head. "Afraid not. You only get one life in this game. You'll have to sit the rest of this out and join the next battle."

Helen sighed and slumped back in her seat. "I so wanted to kill Piers."

"Don't worry. We'll do that for you," Eva said. "You just enjoy the show."

We successfully defeated the giant alien, more by luck than skill on my part. Then it was a race through the cave. I struggled to keep up with Eva as she maneuvered her character skilfully over the obstacles.

"That mountain up ahead is where everyone is heading," Eva said. "We need to make sure Piers doesn't get there."

I jabbed the controller, determined to keep up with Eva. Her character, an enormous, muscled guy with dreadlocks, leaped ahead of me. "How are you making him jump so far?"

"Check the cheat sheet," Eva said. "You need to press a combination of buttons. It will give you super speed."

I looked down at the cheat sheet.

"Look out for that alien," Helen yelled.

I looked up just in time to see an alien about to grab me.

Eva's character turned and shot down the alien.

"Thanks for that," I said, my heart thudding in my chest.

"Maybe stick to running," Eva said. "I'll do the fancy stuff."

My scarred hero ran after Eva's muscled guy. We reached the base of the mountain.

"Wait here. This is the perfect place for an ambush," Eva said.

I stopped my muscled character from moving. "Won't Piers see us?"

"He'll be too busy avoiding being killed by the aliens." Eva pressed a button and changed the view of the game.

I was suddenly looking behind us. Piers's character was speeding toward us, five salivating aliens on his back.

"Are you ready?" Eva didn't even look at me, she was so focused on the game.

I clenched my fingers around the controller. "I'm ready."

Eva changed the view on the game again. Five seconds later, Piers's character rushed past us.

"Now!"

We both shot him in the back. It wasn't the most majestic way to kill an enemy, but it felt good to me.

"You got him!" Helen cheered.

Piers's character lay dead on the ground.

"Now, run!" Eva raced her character up the mountain.

I followed her until we'd shaken off the aliens.

Eva let out a contented sigh. "There's no way he'll live this down. Piers is always bragging about how easy it is to get to Thunder Mountain. Not so easy when you're dead."

"This is a fun way to get back at someone," Helen said. "I need to practice some more."

Eva typed a message and sent it to Piers. *Time for you to go back to playing safe games that don't get you killed.*

We stared at the screen. I expected to see a nasty reply from Piers. There was nothing.

Eva shook her head. "He's gone off-line. Talk about a bad loser."

A second later, a door slammed downstairs.

"Do you think that was Piers?" I was already on my feet, heading to the bedroom door.

"It wouldn't surprise me if he stormed out," Eva said. "He doesn't take defeat well."

As I inched open the door, I could hear murmuring downstairs. I crept along the landing and peered over the banisters. Helen, Flipper, and Eva followed me.

Piers was by the front door. From his tone, he was furious.

Harriet stood with him, her hands on his arms. It looked like she was trying to calm him down.

"They look cozy," Helen whispered.

"They always are," Eva said. "Harriet is supposed to be with Alex, but the way she behaves around Piers, you wouldn't know it."

"Did they used to date?" I asked.

"I don't think so," Eva said. "Piers doesn't like to date. He says it stops other opportunities coming his way. He reckons he's some big-time stud."

Piers turned toward the front door. Harriet pulled him back around and launched herself into his arms.

My mouth fell open as they embraced and kissed passionately.

Eva shook her head. "I should have known. It was only a matter of time before this happened."

"She's cheating on your brother with Piers," Helen whispered. "Shouldn't you stop them?"

"If Alex is idiot enough to be friends with people like this, he's got to expect this kind of thing to happen," Eva said. "Besides, he's not that into Harriet. He just likes the quiet life, so he lets her hang out with him to prevent an argument."

"I wonder how long it's been going on," I said. If Harriet and Piers were close, maybe she was involved in

Greg's death as well. The two of them could have been in on it together.

Eva turned away and walked back to her room. "Harriet chases the money. She'll go wherever it is. Alex isn't giving her enough. She's been whining on about going on holiday for months. He keeps fobbing her off with excuses. I don't think he'd mind the holiday, but I think he'd object to having Harriet hanging on his arm the whole time."

"So, she's after Piers instead?" Helen asked. "Has he got money to give her?"

"His parents have," Eva said. "They fund his lifestyle. Maybe they'll also fund a gold digging girlfriend."

"You don't think much of Harriet," I said.

"I've seen her in action, so I know what she's like," Eva said. "She even made a move on Gregory."

"What happened?" I asked.

"He rejected her, of course," Eva said. "Gregory was an honest guy. He never did anything that might hurt Alex. He was horrified when Harriet made a move on him."

"Were you there when it happened?" Helen asked.

Eva looked at the floor. "I was just passing by, and... happened to see it."

Eva had an uncanny knack for being conveniently behind doors, listening to important conversations. I'd have to be careful of that, in case she caught me talking to Greg's ghost or discussing his murder with Helen.

"How did Harriet take the rejection?" I asked.

"Not well." That evil grin appeared on Eva's face again. "She turned an ugly shade of red and accused him of not liking girls. Of course, he liked girls. Just not girls like Harriet."

"Was Greg seeing anyone before he died?" I asked.

"No, I'd have known if he was," Eva said, her own cheeks turning red. "He never mentioned a girl."

It was clear that Eva had liked Greg. It must have been painful to watch the object of her affection mauled by someone as manipulative as Harriet.

I looked back over the banister and saw Harriet and Piers finally break apart. She glanced over her shoulder before giving him a finger wave and disappearing back into the lounge with Alex.

Piers ran a hand through his hair before turning and leaving the house.

Their relationship added an interesting twist to this mystery. It was possible they were involved in Greg's death and got rid of him together. The fact Harriet had taken an interest in Greg and he'd rejected her was also a motive for her wanting him dead. It sounded like she didn't take rejection well. Whatever the case, I was now very interested in Piers and Harriet.

"Do you want to play some more?" Eva asked. "I'm ready for another game now Piers has gone and can't spoil things."

"Thanks, but I'll pass," I said. "It's getting late. We've got lots to do tomorrow." Like investigating Piers and Harriet and finding out if they were killers.

"You'll have to learn to be a night owl if you get into gaming," Eva said. She glanced at Helen. "Maybe you'd be better sticking to the kitchen. No offense, but you're terrible at playing computer games."

"It was that controller," Helen said. "It doesn't work properly."

Eva grinned. "That must be the problem. I'll see you both tomorrow." She walked into her bedroom and shut the door.

"That was fun," Helen said as we headed to our own rooms.

"You got killed!"

"That was an accident," Helen said. "We got one up on Piers. He was furious when he left."

"Maybe less so after Harriet stuck her tongue down his throat and kissed everything better."

Helen grimaced. "I feel sorry for Alex, but the guy needs a backbone. He should stand up to Harriet and Piers and get rid of them."

"Maybe he doesn't realize what's going on," I said. "He's so caught up in his computer games. And the business is a mess. From what I've seen of the paperwork, he's making plenty of money, but it's off the back of products that are months old. He hasn't created anything new since Greg's death."

"Maybe he's got a creative block." Helen stopped outside my bedroom door. "He can't work without his partner."

"It could be that." I tilted my head as I heard a scratching sound on the other side of the bedroom door. I opened it to find Lucy in the room. "How did she get in here?"

She raised her head and her curly tail wagged just like a dog's.

Flipper bounded over. They sniffed noses before he settled next to her on the floor.

"You can't have a pig in your bedroom," Helen said.

"I don't see why not. She's no worse than Flipper, and he always sleeps with me." I walked over and petted both their heads.

Helen eyed Lucy cautiously. "It's your room. So, what's the plan for tomorrow? Are we going to do more investigating into Piers?"

"I think he's involved. But first, we need to make nice with Harriet," I said. "Find out what she knows about Greg's death and how involved she is with Piers. You never know, we could become her closest friends, and she'll let slip what happened."

Helen's nose wrinkled. "I'd rather take my chances in that alien game for real than befriend Harriet Fawcett."

I laughed. "That's our next move. Speak to Harriet and get the truth out of her. It's time we finally figured out what happened to Greg."

Chapter 12

I woke with a start, fighting the alien that had me in its horrible clutches. I reached around for my gun to shoot it, when I realized the alien was, in fact, my tangled bedsheets.

Groaning, I rolled onto my front. That was the last time I was ever playing violent video games.

I bumped into something warm and soft. Flipper lay next to me in his usual position. By his side was Lucy. I was now sharing my bed with a dog and a pig. I scratched both their heads before reaching for my phone.

I hadn't spoken to Zach since I'd arrived at the house and wanted to know how he was getting on with Amelia. Well, actually, I didn't. It was the reason I hadn't been in touch, other than a brief text message. Zach's ghostly wife was a sore subject. I still wasn't sure how to handle it.

He picked up on the first ring. "Good morning, beautiful."

I smiled when I heard his voice. I missed him, despite the problems with the ghost. "Good morning. I wanted to check-in and let you know how things are going."

"I was going to call you this morning to find out just that. How's life in Kent?"

"I get long lie-ins. I'm making this call from my bed." I wriggled my toes. "I've met two pigs, fought aliens, spent hours playing a game that involved unicorns, and met a ghost."

Zach chuckled. "How many days have you been there?"

"This is my third day," I said. "I know it sounds unusual. My new boss is a gamer. He insisted I play with him."

"Is that in your job description?"

"It falls under *any other duties*," I said. "I don't mind. Alex is a nice guy. I get the impression he's a bit lost since his best friend died."

"This is the ghost you've met?"

"That's right. Greg. I think he was shot."

"Someone killed him?"

"That's what Greg believes," I said. "This might be hard to imagine, but he thinks he was shot by an armed drone. Someone chased him down with it and killed him."

"Is that even possible?" Zach sounded skeptical.

"I don't see why not," I said. "Maybe Gunner knows something about how it would work. Do the police use armed drones?"

"Not that I know of. Hang on a second, let me ask him. I'm putting the phone on speaker." There was the sound of fumbling as Zach adjusted the phone. "Gunner get over here. Lorna wants to ask you something."

"How's it going, Lorna?" Gunner asked a few seconds later.

"Everything's great," I said. "Do you know anything about armed drones?"

"A little. They're used in the military," Gunner said. "Why do you want to know?"

"I think a friend of my boss was killed with an armed drone," I said.

Gunner was silent for a second. "No kidding."

"Are they easy to get hold of?"

"I doubt it," Gunner said. "It's specialist equipment. They're used in battle situations, where it's too dangerous to have soldiers. Sometimes, they're used to scout new locations. You can't buy something like that off the internet."

"Can you make one?"

"If you have the right skills, I guess so," Gunner said. "You do find yourself in some interesting situations."

"It's never my fault," I said. "Ask Zach."

Zach snorted a laugh. "I'm not getting into this. I'd be happy if you stayed home and never worked."

"No, you wouldn't," I said. "That would make me unhappy. I know you wouldn't like that."

Zach sighed. "You're right."

"Maybe we can come down. I can investigate this mysterious armed drone murder," Gunner said.

"Isn't this area out of your jurisdiction?" I asked.

"It wouldn't be anything official," Gunner said. "I can ask around, make a few discreet inquiries. I know a guy who joined the Kent police force a few years back. He might help."

"You'll need to be careful," I said. "A suspect has an uncle who's a sergeant in the local force. I don't want to tip him off that we're on to him."

"I don't deal with sergeants," Gunner said. "I'll go over his head. He won't know a thing."

"Is that the real reason you want to go to Kent?" Zach's tone was teasing.

"I don't know what you're talking about," Gunner said.

I grinned. "If it's any consolation, I'm sure Helen is missing you too."

"I know she is," Gunner said. "We message each other all the time."

"Is that you admitting you're missing Helen bossing you about?" Zach asked.

"I never said that," Gunner grumbled. "It is kind of nice to leave the dishes in the sink and my socks on the floor without getting yelled at."

"I'll make sure not to tell Helen any of that," I said. "If she finds out that's what you're doing, she'll race back and tell you off."

"I also like it when she tells me off," Gunner said.

Zach laughed. "You know, a visit might be nice."

"I am craving some of Helen's triple chocolate brownies," Gunner said.

"We've got a few things to talk about, as well." Zach's tone was now serious.

He was right there. The mysterious Amelia was still very much on my mind. "Why not come down this weekend? We've not looked around much. We can show you the sights, and Gunner can do some discreet investigating."

"That sounds good," Zach said.

Lucy snorted and rolled off the bed with a thud and a squeal.

"Was that Flipper?" Zach asked.

"Erm, no." I watched Lucy as she sniffed the air. "Actually, Flipper's made friends with a pig."

"A pig! Jessie's not going to be happy about that," Zach said. "Flipper is her guy."

"I thought we'd keep quiet about it," I said.

Lucy trotted to the door and shoved it with her snout. Someone needed a toilet break.

"I need to go." I clambered out of bed. "Lucy needs to be let out. I don't want any accidents in the bedroom."

"Hold on a second. You have this pig in your bedroom?" Gunner asked.

I pulled on some clothes and opened the door. "I didn't have much choice. She was here when I came to bed last night. Flipper doesn't mind her being around. She's no trouble. Pigs can be house-trained, just the same as dogs and cats."

"That makes everything all right then," Gunner said. "Zach, I hope you're not thinking of introducing a pig into our household."

"I don't know," Zach said. "If the dogs get along with a pig, it could be fun."

"You'll be looking for a new housemate if we get pigs," Gunner growled.

"Don't worry. Helen's not all that into pigs either. I promise, no pigs will come live with us." I ran down the stairs, following Lucy, Flipper right behind me, and opened the front door to let her out. "So, is that a definite yes to coming this weekend?"

"It is," Zach said. "We'll be there mid-morning."

We said our goodbyes. I felt better for having talked to Zach. We needed to get Amelia dealt with. We could do that together.

I walked around the side of the house to check on Priscilla. As I unlocked the door to the outbuilding, it was shoved from the other side by an eager snout.

Priscilla trotted out, blinking in the daylight. She snorted at me before hurrying to the back door of the main house.

"I'm not sure you can be inside," I said. "Are you house-trained?"

She snorted before vanishing behind a bush. A pig who liked her privacy when it came to toilet duties! I never thought I'd see that.

Priscilla returned a moment later and looked at the door again.

"Well, I guess you can't do too much damage on the tiled floor." I opened the back door and let her in.

Her tail wagged as she trotted in, sat on the door mat, and scratched her rump on the bristles.

I heard footsteps crunching across gravel, and turned to see Harriet skulking around the side of the house. She was doing the walk of shame in yesterday's clothing. Her purse and jacket were clutched to her chest as she made her way toward a white soft top car.

"Flipper, keep an eye on Priscilla. If she causes trouble, just bark," I said.

He cocked his head and then joined Priscilla on the mat.

I hurried toward Harriet, keeping half an eye on both Lucy and Priscilla. "Harriet! You're about early." I suppressed a smile as I saw her bed messy hair and the mascara smudged underneath her eyes.

Harriet turned. Her eyes widened as she saw me. "Oh, you know, I'm always up early." She wrapped her arms around her middle. "Although, I have such a bad headache."

"Maybe you need a coffee." This could be the perfect opportunity to make nice with Harriet and see what she might let slip.

"Yuck! I can't stand the stuff." She rubbed her forehead. "What are you doing out here?"

"I'm on pig duty." I gestured over my shoulder to where Lucy was snuffling under a tree.

Harriet's nose wrinkled. She dropped her purse, phone, and jacket on the ground and sat on a wall. "I don't know why Alex keeps her in the house. I sometimes think he loves her more than me."

"She is a cute pig."

Harriet's eyes narrowed. "Don't go making nice to that pig just to get on Alex's good side."

"I wouldn't do that," I said. This wasn't going how I'd hoped it would. "I just like animals."

Her expression turned sour. "As if you could like that thing. All she does is eat, poop, and make disgusting noises with her snout."

"She's a pig," I said. "What do you expect her to do?"

"I've suggested Alex dress her in cute little outfits," Harriet said. "That would be so much fun, seeing her running around in a tutu with sparkles on her skin."

"Probably not too nice for Lucy, though," I said as Lucy wandered closer. "Pigs aren't used to sparkles and tutus."

"She would be if she were my pig," Harriet said. "When I move in, that's exactly what I'll do. Any animal of mine needs to be pretty."

Lucy snuffled around my feet making cute little snorting noises before sitting by the wall and looking up at us with interest.

"I didn't know you were moving in." I hoped it wasn't happening any time soon. Harriet would delight in playing lady of the manor and bossing me around.

"It won't be long now." Harriet shifted away from Lucy and glanced back at the house. "Alex is dragging his heels. You know how boys are. They need someone to help them make up their minds. I've already moved some of my clothes in and most of my toiletries. He'll get the hint soon enough."

It sounded like Alex was giving his own hints, and they were in the opposite direction.

"It's serious between you and Alex?"

"Of course," Harriet said. "We're together. Why? Don't tell me you're interested in him."

"As an employee, I'm interested in Alex," I said. "I need to make sure his life and business run smoothly."

Her eyes narrowed. "Sure you do. I saw how cozy the two of you were on the couch the other day."

"We were playing a game."

"You're too old to enjoy computer games. I doubt they were even invented when you were born."

Her charm was as endearing as Piers's. I could see why they got along so well. "I think they were."

"It doesn't matter. A word of advice, keep your hands off Alex. He's mine."

I raised my eyebrows. "Alex is my boss, nothing more."

"Don't forget that. He's also young enough to be your son," Harriet said. "I have a feeling you're smarter than you look. I bet you've seen how much money Alex has, and you want some of it."

Smarter than I looked? Was she suggesting I looked like an idiot? "Alex pays me a decent wage. I'm not going to steal from him. I'm also not going to attempt to seduce him in the hope of getting money out of him." I gave Harriet a pointed look. "That never ends well."

Harriet stood and took a step toward me. "You seem to have forgotten yourself. You're an employee here."

"I haven't forgotten that." I could smell Harriet's cloying vanilla perfume.

"Which means I'm practically your boss," Harriet said. "You do what I tell you to."

"You're not my boss." I forced my tone to remain level. "You have nothing to do with Alex's business."

"I will soon enough," Harriet said. "It's only a matter of time before he pays me to be here."

"You want your boyfriend to pay you to stay with him?" Did she have any idea what she'd just made herself sound like?

Harriet huffed. "I mean, he'll have me around a lot more. I'm going to help out with the business. You need to watch yourself. I might be after your position. You might find you're surplus to requirements."

"I'm not sure you're qualified to do what I do."

"I'm more qualified than you think," Harriet snapped. "I could do your job in my sleep."

"You have experience filing end-of-year business accounts, balancing books, transcribing confidential board meeting notes, and arranging multi-destination travel?"

"It all sounds easy enough," Harriet said. "I know how to look after Alex. I know what's best for him."

If she thought that was true, then she was doing a terrible job. Alex was withdrawn, lonely, and isolated.

"In fact, when I come back here later, I'm going to suggest Alex gets rid of you. He didn't want you here in the first place. A bit of nudging from me, and you'll soon be out."

I took a deep breath and let it out calmly. I wouldn't lose this job because of a jealous girlfriend. "If you do that, I might have to mention that I saw you kissing Piers last night."

Harriet's jaw dropped. "I don't know what you're talking about."

"You need to be more discreet if you're going to carry on an affair with Alex's best friend. You really shouldn't have stood in his hallway and made out with Piers. Anyone could have seen you."

Harriet spluttered a few nonsense words. "You've got no proof. If you tell Alex this nonsense, it'll only be more ammunition for me. It shows you're jealous and want me out of the way so you can have Alex all to yourself."

"Maybe so, but it will make Alex suspicious. And you and Piers would have to stop seeing each other until Alex believed you could be trusted. Can you handle that?"

Harriet's lips pinched together. "Don't you dare say anything to him."

"I won't say anything if you don't try to get me fired."

Harriet rolled her eyes. "Fine. You can stay here. For now."

"How kind of you."

She jabbed a finger at me. "Not a word to Alex about any of this. None of it's my fault, anyway."

"How do you figure that?"

Harriet sighed. "It's Piers. He's so good-looking. He's impossible to resist." She giggled and tossed her hair over her shoulder.

"I can see how that would be hard to resist." I shook my head, angry at how fickle she was. "I suppose the fact his family is wealthy has nothing to do with your sudden interest in him."

Harriet jammed her hands on her hips. "Have you ever tried dating poor?"

"Not really, but I don't chase guys because of the amount of money they have in their pockets."

"You should try it. Date a guy with money and everything changes," Harriet said. "Once you get used to a luxury lifestyle, you can never go back. Piers is always generous. Far more than Alex. Alex spends too much money on his business and his stupid games and not enough on me. Piers offered me an opportunity, and I took it. Any smart girl would."

"What about Greg?"

Harriet's brows lowered. "What do you mean? You never met Greg. He's dead."

"I mean, how did you take the fact he rejected your advances when you thought he might be easy to get money from?"

Again, her mouth fell open. "How do you know about that?"

"It's a guess," I said, way past caring about trying to be nice to Harriet. "Greg was a seriously rich guy. You must have been tempted to see if he'd invest his assets in you. If you did do that, he'd have turned you down. It sounds like he was a decent guy. The kind of guy who would never go after his best friend's girl."

"As if any of that is your business." Harriet scowled. "You know nothing about Greg. You also know nothing about Piers and me. If Alex questions me about it, I'll know where the information has come from. I'll make your life a misery if you cross me."

"Providing you stick to your side of the bargain and don't get me fired, I'll do the same," I said.

"Make sure you do." Harriet grabbed her things and stamped away, pulling her jacket on as she did so.

Lucy stood and nudged my leg with her snout. It looked like she was in need of some breakfast, as was I. Arguing with this airhead had made me hungry.

Something glinted on the ground. I bent and picked it up, a smile crossing my face as I realized what I'd discovered. Harriet had left her phone behind.

A quick peek into her private life couldn't do any harm. It might help a lot to figure out how involved she was in Greg's murder.

Chapter 13

Hurrying back inside the house, keeping Harriet's phone out of view in case anyone saw me, I dashed into the kitchen, Lucy, Priscilla, and Flipper hot on my heels.

Harriet's phone could be full of all sorts of secrets. I needed to take a look before she realized she'd left it behind.

I grabbed some leftover food from the fridge and set it on the floor for Lucy, Priscilla, and Flipper to enjoy, before sitting at the kitchen table.

Predictably, the phone was locked with a combination code. I tried turning it off and on again to see if that would help, but it did nothing. The locked screen stared at me.

The kitchen door opened. Alex wandered through, his hair looking as messy as Harriet's. He wore a pair of checked pajama bottoms and a T-shirt with an indie band's name scrawled across it.

He smiled when he saw me. "You're up early."

"So are you," I said. "I had Lucy keeping me company last night. She needed to go out for a comfort break."

Alex smiled affectionately at Lucy as she finished her food. "I heard from Piers you were looking after Priscilla. I'm glad you're all getting along."

"They're good company. Maybe Priscilla can stay here in the long term. She likes Lucy."

"I don't see why not. There's plenty of room. I never thought Piers was into his pig anyway. I'm glad she's here."

I bit the inside of my cheek to stop from telling Alex the truth about Piers and his awful behavior toward Priscilla. "Since you're up early, does that mean we can get started on work before the afternoon?"

He shook his head and grinned. "Not a chance. Harriet woke me up banging around in the bedroom. I decided to grab some food and get started on a game."

"At least give me something to do while you're busy playing," I said.

"What do you fancy doing?"

"You're my boss. You tell me!"

"You can take the day off and start tonight."

I hated that idea. "I'm not much of a night owl. I do my best work first thing in the morning."

Alex pulled out two boxes of cereal and studied the pictures. "It looks like we'll be working different hours."

"Will that be a problem?"

"I don't mind when you work." Alex looked at the phone I had my hand over. "That looks like the latest model."

I tightened my fingers on the phone. "I think it is. But the code is locked."

"You forgot your own pin code?" Alex grabbed milk from the fridge and poured both types of cereal into a bowl.

I shrugged. "It happens to the best of us."

"You need my password app," Alex said. "It securely stores all your passwords. The next time you forget a code, go online, and it does the searching for you."

"That's a great idea."

He smiled ruefully. "I designed it after I kept locking myself out of my own phone."

I knew it was a risk. Alex might recognize this was Harriet's phone. "Is there any chance you can unlock this for me?"

"It shouldn't be a problem," he said around a mouthful of cereal. He placed his bowl down and wandered over, his bare feet padding on the slate tiled floor. "Let's take a look."

I handed Harriet's phone over. If Alex recognized the phone, I would be in big trouble. I hopped up and made myself busy by putting the kettle on to boil and getting my breakfast.

"Here you go." Alex handed me the unlocked phone. "It's permanently unlocked. Just go to your settings when you want to put a new combination code lock on it."

"That's genius." I checked the screen image quickly. There were no obvious pictures on it showing it was Harriet's phone. "How did you do it?"

He smiled and tapped the side of his nose. "It's a trade secret. But you owe me for doing that."

"I'm happy to owe you," I said.

"How about you pay me back straightaway?"

"Doing what?"

"Come and play a game with me."

I grimaced. "I don't think gaming is for me."

"I promise you, it won't be anything violent. Are you any good at racing games?"

"Not really," I said.

"Well, you'll love this new one," Alex said. "You can pick whatever vehicle you want."

"I'm not so sure. There's a lot of paperwork to get through."

"Come on. This is an easy debt to repay." Alex grabbed his bowl of cereal. "One hour of gaming, that's all I ask. Then you're debt free, and can go back to your boring paperwork."

"It's actually *your* boring paperwork."

Alex's grin widened. "Then I insist."

It wasn't a bad offer. I picked up my toast and tea. "Okay, let's go race each other."

We walked into the lounge. Alex got busy loading up the game.

As he did so, I ate my toast and had a discreet look through Harriet's phone. There were loads of selfies of Harriet in all sorts of poses, pouting at the camera and looking over her shoulder with her finger in her mouth. She was quite the lady.

There were also pictures of her dressed up on nights out, and lots of her draped over Alex. There was also a file marked with the letter P. Inside were provocative images of her with Piers.

"It'll be ready to go in a minute," Alex said. "Are you prepared to be beaten on the race track?"

"Well, I was beaten by the Bog Globs, so why not get thrashed on the race track as well?"

Alex smiled. "You never know; racing games could be your thing."

I closed the photos and had a quick look at the messages stored on the phone. A lot of them were receipts of shopping orders or making dates with girlfriends for lunch.

Then I found a new set of messages between Harriet and Piers. I scanned them. They discussed a deal and the need to keep it quiet about it.

My blood chilled as I continued up the message stream. They mentioned having to keep Greg quiet and that he knew too much.

This was the proof I needed that Piers and Harriet had killed Greg.

"What's going on in here?" Camilla strode into the lounge and glared at Alex. "I hope you're not planning on wasting your morning on some ridiculous game."

"No, I was going to do some important fact-finding research on a new release from a rival company," Alex said.

Camilla tutted and shook her head. "Your important research will have to wait. I need company at the airfield. I'm volunteering there today."

Alex groaned and slumped into his seat. "Can't you find somebody else? Why not take Eva?"

"No, I want my son to come with me," Camilla said. "Eva won't enjoy the planes."

"And I will?"

"Of course!"

"How about Lorna?" Alex sounded desperate. "I bet she loves planes."

"Lorna's far too busy sorting out your mess of a business to spend time on planes," Camilla said with a swift nod in my direction.

Alex gestured at the screen. "This is important."

"It might be, but it can also wait," Camilla said. "You're coming with me."

Alex turned his pleading gaze to me.

There was nothing I could do. I shrugged him an apology. "I'll get to work on the filing."

"That's a perfect idea." Camilla turned and left the room. "Alex, you need to get dressed. I'll see you in the car in five minutes."

He groaned again.

Sometimes, he really acted like a big kid. "What does your mom do at the airfield?"

He pulled himself to his feet, his shoulders slumped. "Nothing exciting. It's full of boring planes. I'd better go. Mom gets mad if I'm late." He skulked out of the room, leaving me with the racing game flashing on the screen, asking if I was ready to burn rubber.

I picked up the controller, not sure how to turn it off.

A black box appeared on the screen. *Mickey Kill would like to make contact.*

I looked at the controller and pressed the okay button. What did Mickey Kill have to say to me?

"How are you, Lorna?" That same robotic voice he'd used the first time we'd spoken sounded through the speakers.

"I'm fine, thanks."

"I'm glad to hear that. Do you want to play a flying game?"

I shrugged. I didn't really. "I've got lots to do today. Maybe another time."

"You're wearing yesterday's clothes."

Looking down at my hastily pulled on clothes, I blushed. He was right. I was a little weirded out by the fact he could see me. "I had to let Lucy out in a hurry this morning. I grabbed the first thing I could find."

"When a pig has got to go, a pig has got to go." Mickey Kill was quiet for a few seconds. "So, do you want to play?"

Five minutes wouldn't hurt, and I might be able to get more information out of Mickey Kill about Greg. "You need to tell me what to do."

"It's easy," Mickey Kill said. "Just make sure you don't crash."

I watched as the screen changed. I was looking through the cockpit of a plane in the air. "Have you any hints about what I'm supposed to do so I don't crash?"

"Do you see the red line in the right-hand corner?"

"I do."

"Keep it level," he said. "Avoid any mountains. And you might occasionally get shot at, so dodge the bullets."

"Are you going to shoot at me?"

"We're on the same side," came his reply. "How's your investigation going?"

I hesitated. It felt weird sharing information with a complete stranger, but I was interested in his theories.

"You can trust me," Mickey Kill said. "I know a lot about Greg. I want to make sure his killer gets what they deserve."

My plane veered rapidly off-course and an alarm sounded. I pressed the buttons randomly on the controller. "What am I doing wrong?"

"Keep the red line in the center," Mickey Kill reminded me.

The plane dived toward the ground. I'd lost control. "I think Greg was killed by Harriet and Piers." I watched as my plane exploded in a fiery mess.

"You lose," Mickey Kill said.

"It was my first try," I said. "I bet you crashed the first time you played this game."

"I'm always good," he replied. "At all games."

"Maybe we can meet. You can share gaming tips and tell me what you know about Greg's killer."

There was silence. It looked like I'd shocked Mickey Kill.

"Have you disappeared?" I asked.

"I never meet people," Mickey Kill said. "It's better that way."

"For who?"

"For me," he said. "The gaming world is a dodgy place."

I'd heard that before. "I promise you, I'm safe to be around. You said I needed to trust you. Well, you need to do the same with me if you really want to help Greg."

Another silence stretched out. "The house you're living in is dangerous. Please be careful. I'd hate to see either you or Helen get hurt."

My pulse sped up. "Dangerous! What makes you say that?"

"There are powerful forces at work there."

"Powerful forces?"

The door behind me banged open, and I jumped. Helen, Flipper, Lucy, and Priscilla appeared.

"What are you doing in here on your own?" Helen asked. "I found these three in the kitchen trying to knock the trash over and eat the contents."

I looked back at the screen. "I was just... talking to someone."

Helen looked around. "There's no one here."

She was right. Mickey Kill had vanished, leaving me with more questions than answers, and an unsettled feeling in my stomach.

Chapter 14

"Where did you get to so early?" Helen asked as I followed her back to the kitchen with Lucy, Priscilla, and Flipper. "I checked in your room when I got up, but it was empty."

"I went outside with Lucy," I said. "And I met Harriet sneaking out whilst I was outside."

"I bet she was her usual charming self." Helen made toast and a pot of tea for us both.

"She was a delight. Harriet thinks I'm interested in Alex."

Helen laughed. "I can see you chasing Alex around the lounge, trying to get your claws into him."

"I could be someone's sugar mommy if I wanted to be."

"I never said you couldn't." Helen joined me at the table, poured the tea, and set out the preserves. "I'm not sure what Zach would have to say about that, though."

"Talking of Zach," I said, "he's coming down here at the weekend with Gunner."

"I know," Helen said. "Gunner sent me a message."

"Wow! He is keen. In fact, he was the one who suggested they come down. That guy has it bad for you."

"So he should," Helen said. "I'm fabulous."

I couldn't argue with that. "Getting back to Harriet, she accidentally left behind her phone. I accidentally got

Alex to break the code and then accidentally looked at all her photos and messages."

Helen's eyes widened. "What did you discover?"

"That she wanted Greg out of the way," I said. "Piers is also involved. I found a long series of messages saying that Greg knew too much and needed to be kept quiet."

"That sounds dark," Helen said.

"There was also mention of a business deal."

"Maybe it's the dating app Alex created. Have you got any idea how much he sold it for?"

"There's an easy way to find out." I pulled out my phone and scrolled through business news sites.

"I'm guessing ten million," Helen said.

I nearly choked on my tea when I found the real amount. "This is ridiculous."

"Go on, make me feel sick. Tell me how much."

"Alex sold the dating app for sixty-four million."

Helen licked strawberry jelly off her fingers. "No wonder Harriet and Piers wanted to get their hands on it."

"I'm not sure this is the business deal they're talking about," I said. "Neither of them are business partners with Alex. I've seen the contracts and all the business paperwork. They're not mentioned in any of it. Alex only ever worked with Greg."

"Then they're just as we originally thought," Helen said. "Fake friends chasing Alex for his money and killing off the competition."

Eva walked in, her expression fierce. "You've got that right. Don't trust either of them."

I almost wasn't surprised to discover she'd been listening at the kitchen door. "What makes you say that?" I gestured to the pot of tea.

Eva nodded and sat at the table. "Neither of them is clever enough to come up with their own successful business, so they sponge off my brother."

I grabbed another mug and poured her some tea. "You don't think Piers and Harriet are being honest with Alex?"

"Not for a second. You saw them making out. That's not the kind of thing you do if you're a decent human being."

"Do you have any proof Piers and Harriet are just here for the money?"

"Other than the fact they behave like spoiled idiots who always have their hands out, no." Eva looked from me to Helen. "I have to ask, why are you both so interested in them?"

A shiver ran down my spine. I didn't need to look around to know Greg had appeared. I was glad he was here. I was beginning to think he'd vanished for good.

"I don't like to think of a decent guy being mistreated," I said. "It sounds like they were horrible to Greg."

Eva set her mug down and looked at the table. "I miss him. I know he didn't think much of me. He never noticed when I was around. No matter what I did or the clothes I wore, he was only ever interested in the business."

"He could have been shy," Helen said. "Guys can be daft when they're really into a girl. It took my Gunner ages to open up and say how much he liked me. Before that, all we did was fight."

Eva shrugged. "It's too late to do anything about it now. I could have paraded in front of him with an enormous banner saying *I love you*, and he wouldn't have realized it was for him."

Greg drifted to the edge of the table. His eyes were wide as he stared at Eva. It looked like he really had no clue she'd liked him.

I decided to let her into our confidence. She was a suspect, but I didn't have her at the top of the list. "What do you know about the drone that shot Greg?"

Eva looked up. "Not much. It was all kept quiet. I never saw it. I never pay much attention to what goes on at the airbase."

"You wouldn't know if it could be used to target someone?"

Her brows lowered, and she chewed on her black painted lips. "Well, I guess it could. They normally need an operator. Alex would know more about that than me."

"Alex owns a drone?" Helen asked.

"No. He's just stupidly smart and knows about everything. Not that you'd think it to look at him. He hides his smarts well." Eva stared at me. "Why are you asking about the drone?"

I glanced at Helen, and she nodded. "Would you be shocked if I suggested someone used the drone to target Greg?"

Eva's mouth opened. She blinked several times before swallowing. "I did wonder. I mean, everyone said it was a horrible accident. How hard can it be to fly one of those things? It's designed by the military. They shouldn't get something that basic so wrong."

"You think it's a possibility?" I asked.

Eva nodded. "We got a weird visit from the head guy at the airbase. He said it was an accident. The drone was being tested on a night flight when it malfunctioned. Greg was in the wrong place at the wrong time. I didn't trust the military guy, though. He got all shifty when I started asking questions."

"What kind of questions?" I asked.

"I wanted to know who was piloting the drone," Eva said. "Maybe they weren't competent and had made an error."

"He didn't think that was possible?"

"That's the weird thing. He wouldn't give me a straight answer. He said the drone had been checked and had an engineering fault that would be rectified. It wasn't a user based error, apparently."

"Maybe someone was using the drone when they shouldn't have been," Helen said. "If that leaked out, the base would be in trouble. People could lose their jobs."

"They should," Eva said. "Compensation and improved security won't bring Gregory back."

"It must be someone connected to the military base," Helen said. "Did Greg have any enemies who work there?"

"He didn't have any enemies," Eva said, "and no connections to the base."

"Sneaking into a military airbase and using a drone to kill someone wouldn't have been easy," I said.

"If you're a local it's super easy," Eva said. "Maybe stealing the drone isn't, though. I'm guessing those things are locked away. But getting in is possible. We did it a couple of times when we first got here. There's nothing interesting there, though. Do you really think someone used a drone to target Gregory?"

"I have a gut feeling something bad happened." I looked at Greg. "Someone didn't want Greg around."

"Lorna has great gut instincts," Helen said. "You should listen to her."

Eva nodded. "I am. I can see it in her aura. She's telling the truth."

I raised my eyebrows. Maybe there was something to this aura business. "It's not too late to help Greg. That's why we're interested."

"I overheard you talking about Harriet and Piers," Eva said. "Do you think they're involved?"

Greg gave me a startled look and moved closer.

"I think so," I said. "Maybe Harriet tried to get her hands on Greg's money, and it went wrong."

"Harriet's spiteful and shallow, but she wouldn't have a clue how to fly a drone. She'd be too worried about breaking a nail," Eva said. "And as for Piers, he's too lazy."

"He could have hired someone to pilot the drone," Helen said.

"Piers acts like the big man, but he's nothing more than a coward," Eva said. "He wouldn't have the first clue how to hire someone to kill Gregory. He'd think it would be like in the movies, where you dial an anonymous number and transfer money into a secret bank account. He'd be far too scared about getting caught and going to prison. I doubt they do his kind of designer brand hair gel behind bars. Piers always likes to look his best."

I looked at Greg and could still see the shock on his face. I didn't know whether it was because of Eva's revelation that she loved him or because it was the first time he'd considered Harriet and Piers as his killers.

"You're both going to think I'm crazy for saying this, but sometimes, I think Gregory is still in this house," Eva said quietly.

I glanced at Helen. "What makes you think that?"

"I've always considered myself a sensitive," Eva said. "I pick up on good and bad vibes. And, as you know, I also see people's auras. I can't be sure, but I see movement out of the corner of my eye. When I turn and look, it's gone. It's as if someone was there and blinked out of sight just before I saw them."

"Like a ghost someone?" Helen said cautiously.

Greg drifted closer to Eva, and she shuddered.

"I don't know if I believe in ghosts," Eva said. "Anyway, why would Gregory want to hang around here?"

"Because he has unfinished business," I said. "If we're right, and something bad happened to him, then he'd want to put that right before moving on."

"I'm probably being daft. I miss him so much that I'm willing him to be around." Eva raised her head and appeared to stare directly at Greg before sighing and taking another drink from her mug. "I'm glad you're both here. I can't talk to Alex about it. He'd think it was weird me liking his best friend."

"Can you talk to your mom?" I asked. "She might understand."

"Mom doesn't believe in love," Eva said. "You might have noticed a distinct lack of a husband around."

"I wondered where Mr. Hudson was," I said.

"Serving on the other side of the world in the military. He's as far away from her as he can be. They don't get along. Mom always says I have to have a career before I marry. She said no woman should go into marriage without having skills behind her in case she gets abandoned."

"That's sensible advice," I said. "If you meet the right guy, he won't mind you having a career. If he does, he's not the right one for you."

"Are you married?" Eva asked.

"She's not married yet," Helen said, before I had a chance to respond. "A proposal isn't far away, though."

I waved my hand at Helen. "I'm not married, and I'm not sure about the proposal. I have been seeing the same guy for a while."

"He's happy with what you do?" Eva asked. "He doesn't mind you going away to work?"

I tilted my head from side to side. Zach didn't love what I did. He didn't mind me doing the personal assistant side of things. He wasn't so keen on the ghosts. "Zach understands. He knows I need to do this, and he respects that."

"You're lucky," Eva said. "Although, I reckon if I'd gotten Gregory to notice me, he'd have been that sort of guy. Caring, sweet, and supportive."

Greg rested a hand on Eva's shoulder. A look of sadness crossed his face.

We needed to focus on him and not our messy love lives. "If you don't think Piers and Harriet were involved in Greg's death, who else could it be?"

"How about Mickey Kill?" Helen said. "Anyone with a name like that has to be up to no good."

"The gamer? The guy no one has ever met?" Eva asked.

"I've spoken with him on the computer," I said. "He's really violent in the games he plays. Maybe that violence spilled over into real life."

"No way," Eva said. "Mickey Kill is a phantom. Gregory never met him. I bet he's some nerdy kid with glasses who's still in high school. He can't be involved in this."

My phone buzzed. I picked it up and saw a message from an unknown number.

I am not a phantom.

I showed the message to Helen.

"Are you serious? Mickey Kill has your number?" Helen stared at me with wide eyes.

"I never gave it to him. I have no clue how he got it, or how he heard us talking just now." I looked around the kitchen, feeling seriously creeped out.

"He's a hacker. He can get into any computer system, so he says." Eva shrugged. "Your phone would have been easy."

My phone buzzed again. *I'm serious. You all need to be careful.*

I showed them the message.

"If you're so serious," I said, "why don't we meet? You can give us your theories about what happened to Greg. You can also prove your innocence."

My phone went silent.

"You see!" Eva slapped a hand on the table. "Mickey Kill is a joke."

"Okay, so if it's not Piers and Harriet and it's not the elusive Mickey Kill, who would you have as a suspect?" I asked.

Eva looked at the floor and dropped her hands into her lap. "I have someone in mind. I don't like to say, though."

I sat forward in my seat. "Go on. Who do you think killed Greg?"

Eva licked her lips. "There's only one person I know who is smart enough to control an armed drone."

"Who's that?" Helen asked.

"My brother. Alex."

Chapter 15

I shook my head. Alex was too much of a nice guy to be involved in this. "Why do you think that?"

"Alex is a genius," Eva said. "He can do anything he sets his mind to."

"That doesn't mean he killed Greg," Helen said. "They were best friends."

Greg nodded and spun around the table. Flipper ran along behind him.

I discreetly gestured them both to stop before Greg turned the kitchen icy cold.

"It's more than that," Eva said, her gaze following Flipper. "Alex used to do contract work for the military."

"What kind of work?" I asked.

"I don't know the details," Eva said. "It was hush-hush. I used to question him about it, but he never revealed what he was up to. He said he couldn't talk about it."

"You found out?" Helen asked.

"I followed him one day and watched what he was up to."

"What was he doing?" I said.

"He was remote flying drones."

My eyes widened. "The same drone that killed Greg?"

"I'm not sure," Eva said. "That's what he did for the military. He provided them with blueprints to design drones that could be piloted long distance. It wouldn't be difficult to add a weapon to the drone and go after Gregory."

"Your brother tested the armed drone on Greg?" I still couldn't get my head around that idea.

"He had access to it," Eva said.

"Why would he do that?"

"They were in business together," Eva said. "Maybe they had a falling out. Maybe Gregory decided he wanted the business for himself."

Greg stopped dead and frowned. Flipper ran straight through him, jumped around, and shook himself.

"Did you ever hear them arguing?" I asked.

"No, but Alex had the tools to kill Greg. It has to be him," Eva said.

"Could your brother have been suspicious about Greg and Harriet?" Helen asked. "Harriet was interested in Greg. You told us he gave her the brush off. Maybe that's the reason Alex was angry at Greg. He thought he was trying to steal his girlfriend."

"I don't think he'd have minded," I said. "Alex isn't keen on Harriet."

"Who would be?" Eva's expression darkened. "She's a parasite, feeding off anyone who'll let her get close enough. Greg was smart enough to see that and turn her down."

"I just don't see Alex doing something like this," I said.

"He gets obsessed with things," Eva said. "It's the reason his apps and games are such a success. He works on them until it almost kills him. Everything has to be right. Once he gets an idea in his head, he won't leave it alone."

As much as I hated to admit it, Eva could be onto something. Alex was super smart and really into his gaming. And we'd just discovered he could pilot an armed drone and would have had access to one. Despite all that, I still wasn't convinced.

My phone vibrated. I looked down and saw another message.

Don't trust her. She's only jealous.

I glanced at Eva. She could be jealous. Alex was the golden boy in the family. He made all the money and was the reason for their success. Could Eva be trying to frame her brother? Was she jealous of him and wanted him out of the way?

"We still need to focus on Piers and Harriet," I said. "There's evidence suggesting they were involved."

"How about the evidence that my brother has the skills to fly a drone?" Eva asked.

Helen raised her eyebrows at me. "Eva has a point. We shouldn't discount Alex because you like working for him."

"It's not that." Well, it sort of was. My phone buzzed again.

Eva's leading you away from the real suspects.

"Is that Mickey Kill?" Eva's eyes narrowed as she looked at my phone.

"No. It's my boyfriend." My phone buzzed again.

You're not my type.

Charming! I was saving him from another embarrassing put down from Eva, and he was insulting me.

We need to meet.

Eva stood and walked to the door. "I was wasting my time telling you what I know." She pulled open the door and disappeared before I had a chance to say anything.

I was grateful for her information, but was more confused than ever.

"Exactly who is messaging you?" Helen asked. "That wasn't Zach, was it?"

"It's still Mickey Kill. He wants to meet. He told me not to trust Eva."

"Do you?"

I looked at Greg, who appeared as confused as I felt. "Right now, I have no clue who to trust."

My nerves made me jumpy as I finished work for the day. I'd arranged to meet with Mickey Kill at a cafe in the next village, and really didn't know what to expect.

The arrangements had been odd. We were to sit at a specific table and not leave until he'd made contact.

I hurried out the front door to find Helen already waiting beside the car. Flipper hopped into the back seat, and we set off for our meeting with Mickey Kill.

"I wonder who this guy is," Helen said. "He could be a criminal mastermind, wanted by MI5 for crimes against the government."

"I'm more interested in what he's going to tell us about who killed Greg. I also want to know how he can listen to our conversations all the time."

"He must have the house bugged."

"There have to be cameras he can access as well."

"He'd better not have any of those cameras in my bedroom. I'm not giving this guy a free peep show every time he fancies a look."

"It might be worth checking your room, just in case."

"I bet he's using our phones," Helen said. "They all have cameras. So do most computers. If Mickey Kill is as good as he reckons he is, it wouldn't be hard for him to hack through the systems and see what's going on. I'll be keeping my phone flipped over, so he can't make use of the camera when I'm getting dressed."

"It's all a bit creepy."

"It's super creepy," Helen said. "What do you expect from a guy who calls himself Mickey Kill?"

We drove through the countryside for fifteen minutes until we passed the village sign for Badger's Copse. Neat rows of cottages sat back from the road, the cheery amber glow of lights from the windows not improving my nervousness.

"This is the place." Helen parked outside the Teapot Cafe. The building was whitewashed. Tubs of early spring flowers lined the walkway to the cafe door.

"This looks surprisingly normal for a criminal mastermind," I said.

"That's why he's so good at what he does," Helen said. "He's a master of disguise. No one would expect an international villain to use a cute little place like this as their base."

I arched an eyebrow. "Mickey Kill is now an international villain?"

"He could be." Helen grinned at me. "Hopefully, we can get ourselves something nice to eat while we're here. At least then, it won't have been a complete waste of time if Mickey Kill turns out to be a spotty youth with poor social skills."

"Maybe Mickey Kill is onto something. He has an eerie knack for knowing what's going on. He could have seen something on the cameras when he was spying on the family."

I looked at Flipper, who was in the back seat, his ears up. "Sorry, boy. You'll have to sit this one out. The cafe owner won't want you in there shedding fur all over the lovely food."

Flipper's ears lowered.

"I promise I'll bring you a tasty treat." I left the window open so he had plenty of fresh air, before leaving the car with Helen.

I pushed open the cafe door. The welcoming smell of warm bread drifted up my nose.

A smiley-faced middle-aged man was behind the counter. He nodded a greeting as he walked over to the table where Mickey Kill had told us to sit.

Helen snatched up a menu and studied it intently. From the growing smile on her face, it looked like there were plenty of treats for her to choose from.

"What can I get you?" the man asked. He took out a pen and pad.

"We'll have a pot of English breakfast tea, a slice of triple chocolate brownie, and some pecan pie." Helen looked over at me. "What are you going to have?"

"You're having two cakes?"

"Of course! I always have to try the local produce."

I shook my head as I scanned the menu. Why was I not surprised? "I'll have the apple danish."

"Excellent choices, ladies." The man wrote down our order. "I'll be right back."

I looked around the cafe. There was only one couple in there, an elderly man and woman drinking hot chocolate and reading the paper.

"Unless Mickey Kill is the old guy in the corner," Helen whispered, "he's not here yet."

"He could be in disguise." I glanced at the couple again. If he was in disguise, it was an excellent one.

Ever since Eva had revealed her belief that Alex had killed Greg, I'd felt uncertain. I'd been so sure it was Piers and Harriet, but how had they gotten their hands on an armed drone?

"This could be him," Helen whispered, bringing me out of my thoughts.

The door to the cafe opened. A man in a smart navy suit strode through. He headed to the counter and talked to the man behind it.

"He looks too normal," I said.

"Again, it could be an amazing disguise," Helen said.

We both watched the man as he bought a drink.

He glanced over and saw us watching.

I grabbed the menu and hid behind it.

"Very subtle," Helen muttered.

"I don't want him to think we're weird."

"It's too late for that. You've scared him off."

I peeked over the top of the menu to see the man hurry out of the cafe with his drink. "Of course he's scared. Two strange women were eyeing him up."

The server returned with a tray and placed the tea and cakes on the table.

"These look good," Helen said.

"Thank you. My wife makes them fresh every day," the man said. "She loves nothing more than trying out a new cake recipe." He patted his rotund stomach.

Helen sampled the pecan pie. "This is incredible."

"I'll pass the compliments to the chef." The server smiled before returning to the counter.

We spent a few minutes sampling all the cakes. They were mouth wateringly tasty.

I'd almost forgotten the reason we were here when the cafe door opened and a tall, skinny boy of about fifteen approached us. His cheeks colored as he looked at Helen and he stumbled over his feet. It was a reaction that happened to many men, young or old, the first time they saw Helen and her curves.

"Can we help you?" I asked.

"I've got a message for you." He glanced at Helen again and looked away.

I repressed a smile. "Who's the message from?"

"Mickey."

"You know Mickey?" I asked.

"I'm his contact." His blush deepened.

"What's the message?"

"It's all to do with the business."

"The business?" That wasn't terribly helpful. "Whose business?"

"The... I forget some of the message. Something was stolen. There was a game involved. Does that make sense?"

I looked at Helen, and she shrugged.

"Not really," I said. "Who gave you this message? We can ask him what he means."

The boy cleared his throat. "I'll try again. The plan was stolen. The business plan, I think."

"You're sure that's the whole message?" Helen asked.

The boy glanced at her. His gaze drifted to her cleavage. "I think so."

Helen sighed and folded her arms across her chest. "Tell us who gave you this message."

His eyes snapped up, and he blinked. "I can't."

"Why not?"

"I was told not to."

"Who told you not to tell us?" Helen looked around the cafe. "Are they in here?"

"No." The boy looked over his shoulder out onto the street.

I looked out the window and saw a man sitting astride a bicycle. He had a black cap on his head, the brim pulled down low, so I couldn't see his face.

"He's out there, isn't he?" I was on my feet and hurrying out the door.

"Wait! I never told you it was him," the boy said.

As I got closer, I noticed the bike rider had a scarf over the lower half of his face and dark glasses on. He couldn't have made himself any more conspicuous if he'd tried.

"Don't you dare run away!" I ran toward him as he tried to peddle off and grabbed his jacket. "You're Mickey Kill." I struggled with him for a few seconds before his bike unbalanced and he fell off.

"I didn't tell them anything," the boy said as he reached my side. Helen was right behind him, still chewing on a piece of pie.

Mickey Kill struggled onto his knees. "Why did you attack me?" His voice was muffled behind the scarf.

"Because we need answers," I said. "The message you gave this boy was rubbish. It didn't make any sense."

Mickey Kill's shoulders slumped. He turned his head toward the boy. "I repeated the message to you three times. You said you'd got it."

"You mumble," the boy said. "I only got about half of it."

Mickey Kill climbed to his feet. "Then I'm not paying you."

"Come off it," the boy said. "I did what you asked."

"You did the opposite," Mickey Kill said. "You led them right to me."

"Just pay him," Helen snapped. "We need to talk to you about important business."

Mickey Kill sighed before shoving his hand into his pocket and thrusting a note at the boy.

"You're a bunch of weirdos." He grabbed it and ran off, without looking back.

I placed my hands on my hips as my gaze ran over Mickey Kill. "Are you going to take off your disguise?"

"I don't like people seeing my face."

"We're not going to tell your mom you've been out after curfew if that's what you're worried about," Helen said.

"I don't live with my mom!"

"So you won't mind if we see your face," I said.

Reluctantly, Mickey Kill lowered the scarf and removed the dark glasses. He had a narrow face, pale skin, and large dark eyes.

Now I could see his face, I wasn't so worried. He was young and nervous. "It's nice to meet you in person, Mickey Kill. What's with all the secrecy?"

Mickey shuffled his feet. "I've already said that place you're working in is dangerous. It's risky being involved in this."

"We are involved," I said. "We're working with Alex."

"Alex isn't the problem," Mickey Kill said. "He's a decent guy. Not as good a gamer as me, of course, but he's fair about stuff."

"We don't care about your games," Helen said. "What do you know about how Greg was killed?"

Mickey Kill shushed Helen. "Not so loud. People might be listening."

"Like you do, using my phone," I said.

Mickey Kill shrugged. "I needed to know I could trust you."

"You can," I said. "We want to figure out what happened to Greg. What was the message you wanted to give us?"

Mickey Kill looked up and down the empty street before stepping closer. "Piers and Harriet stole a business. They betrayed Greg."

"What did they do with the stolen business?" I asked.

"They gave it to Alex," Mickey Kill said. "Greg had been working on a new version of a dating app. It was different to what Alex already has. It was next level sophisticated. He was willing to offer a one hundred percent guarantee you would find your soulmate using this app."

"That sounds too good to be true," I said.

"It really wasn't," Mickey Kill said. "I've seen the prototype."

"Why would Greg keep this new app from Alex?"

"He wasn't planning to," Mickey Kill said. "He wanted to make sure it was perfect before he unveiled it. They were good friends, but their friendship was a competitive one. They were always trying to outdo each other and produce a better game or app."

"Piers and Harriet found out about it?" Helen asked.

"They must have. I watched Piers play nice with Greg and heard them talking about the dating app. Greg showed him an early version of what he was working on. When Greg left the room, Piers accessed his data and made a copy."

"Has Alex seen this data?" I asked.

"Not yet," Mickey Kill said. "Piers gave it to him, but Alex is too wrapped up in finishing his Bog Glob game to look through it. The guy gets crazy into something and that's all he can focus on."

"Which means Piers's plan has failed," I said. "If Piers stole this information off Greg to impress Alex and make him think this was his design but Alex isn't using it, then what's he achieved?"

"Alex will get around to it," Mickey Kill said.

"Is that why Piers is still hanging about?" I asked. "He's waiting for Alex to see what a great concept he's given him and reward him?"

Mickey Kill nodded. "I reckon Piers thinks Alex will see how incredible this prototype is and bring in Piers as an official business partner. When he does that, he'll be wealthy beyond his wildest dreams. Piers has his eyes on the money and is prepared to wait."

"But if Piers only has this one amazing app, won't Alex realize something is off?" Helen asked.

"Piers won't care," Mickey Kill said. "He'll take the money and run."

"Is Harriet involved as well?" I asked.

"She must be," Mickey Kill said. "Do you know that they're seeing each other behind Alex's back?"

"I've seen them together," I said.

"Don't trust either of them," Mickey Kill said. "I'm sure they killed Greg to keep him quiet. He must have figured out what Piers did and was going to tell Alex."

"How would they have access to an armed drone?"

"Maybe it was a setup," Mickey Kill said.

"You mean they didn't use an armed drone?" I was getting confused.

"All I know is it has to be them."

The man in the cafe opened the door and looked out at us. "Is everything okay?"

"Yes, sorry to abandon our food," I said. "We saw an old friend and wanted to say hello."

"Your tea's getting cold," the man said. "I'll make you a fresh pot."

"Thanks," Helen said. "That will be lovely."

"Why don't you come inside with us?" I said to Mickey Kill. "We can talk about this some more. We need to figure out how Piers or Harriet got hold of an armed drone."

Mickey looked over his shoulder and shook his head. "I can't afford to be seen out in public for too long. There are eyes everywhere watching what we do. This street has closed circuit cameras."

"For our safety, not to spy on us," I said, looking around the peaceful street.

"That's what they want you to believe."

"For goodness sake," Helen said, "anyone would think you're a wanted criminal."

Mickey Kill flashed her a smile. "Maybe I am."

She gave a disparaging snort. "I doubt it. You don't look old enough to shave, let alone commit a crime."

Mickey Kill pouted. "You've seen me in action on the games."

"Shooting people in a computer game doesn't make you a hard-core gangster."

Mickey Kill grabbed his bike from the ground. "There's a killer on the loose. I don't want to be around in case they get suspicious that we're working out what they did and come after me."

"A true sign of a wanted criminal," Helen said. "Scared to be out after dark."

"Wait! You need to help us," I said. "We need proof about Harriet and Piers."

"All I can tell you is what I saw." Mickey Kill jumped on his bike.

"How are you able to see what we do inside Alex's house?" Helen asked. "It's full on creepy that you're watching us."

He smiled. "We all have our secrets."

Helen tutted and shook her head. "Stop spying. It's rude."

"If I wasn't spying, then I wouldn't know something was off with Harriet and Piers." Mickey Kill shot off, leaving us standing outside the cafe.

"He wasn't much help," Helen said.

"Not much," I said. "I was expecting him to give us some actual proof, not more theories."

Helen looked back at the cafe. "Come on. We've got tea to drink, and I want to try a strawberry tarte. Maybe that will help us figure out this mess."

I highly doubted it, but felt in need of caffeine and sugar. My head was full of suspects and questions, and I felt no closer to helping Greg.

Chapter 16

We were the last customers to leave the cafe, having sampled several more cakes.

I had a bag of cakes in my hand, one with Flipper's name on it. It was only right he got a treat after we'd left him alone for so long.

I sat in the back seat of the car with Flipper and fed him pieces of sponge cake as Helen drove us back to the house.

"We need to get this sorted out," Helen said.

"It will be good to help Greg," I said. "The poor guy doesn't have a clue what's going on. When he does appear, he's either too glum to help or gets spooked and vanishes."

"A ghost who gets scared," Helen said. "Now I've seen everything."

I smiled. "You can't actually see Greg."

"You know what I mean. Besides, I'm not that bothered about Greg," Helen said. "Gunner and Zach arrive in two days. I don't want to be distracted by trying to solve this murder."

"It would be terrible if an unsolved crime impeded your love life."

Helen shot me a dirty look in the rear-view mirror. "You should want it sorted quickly as well. Gunner never knows what to make of your ghost talk, and Zach never likes it when you get your head turned by an unquiet spirit."

"Zach's used to it," I said, "especially now he has his own resident ghost at our house to deal with. And as for Gunner, well, he can think what he likes about ghosts, so long as he doesn't make fun of me about it."

"He'd never do that," Helen said. "He believes you. Gunner's very open-minded."

"Is that in all aspects of his life?"

"Don't be rude!"

I sat back in the seat and fed Flipper the last of the cake. Now he had sponge cake in his belly, he was happy.

I let out a sigh and looked out the window. The unfinished business of Zach's ghostly ex-wife troubled me. I needed time off to sort that out. It made me uncertain of everything I'd built with Zach. That wasn't fair on either of us.

Helen glanced over her shoulder. "Is everything okay?"

I ran my fingers through Flipper's fur. "I'm worried about Amelia."

"You'll get that figured out," she said. "There must be a reason she's living in our home."

"That reason is Zach."

"He doesn't love her," Helen said. "He's crazy about you. I know he's not great at showing it, but he's happy."

"I know he cares," I said. "I just wish he hadn't kept it a secret from me. Now she's in the house and causing us problems. At least if I'd known he'd been married, and then the ghost wife popped up, it wouldn't have been such a shock."

"Don't let her cause problems between you two," Helen said. "When we get back from this job, tell

Amelia to get lost. She's not welcome. Can't you get her exorcised?"

"I've never done an exorcism. I don't think it's the right fit for a ghost. She's not a demon or anything negative."

"She's hardly a positive influence on your relationship with Zach," Helen said. "You and Amelia need to sit down and figure out what she's playing at. Tell her she's had her chance with Zach and messed up. It's time for her to move on."

"Maybe she can't move on," I said. "Maybe she's stuck here and needs help."

"She's come to you for help?"

"That's part of the problem. Amelia never appears when I'm around. If she wants my help, then she's rubbish at asking for it."

"It could be she's just a spiteful ex-wife with an attitude," Helen said. "Make sure she doesn't walk all over your relationship with Zach. The two of you are so good together. Don't let Amelia spoil things."

"You're right. Not only about Amelia but also Greg. It'll be good to sort this all out. We still need evidence that Harriet and Piers were involved in his death. I'm not convinced it was Alex, despite what Eva told us."

A small, low-flying aeroplane droned past us, heading toward the ground.

"That might be going to the place where Camilla volunteers," I said.

"What does she do there?"

"Nothing exciting from what I've heard about the place," I said. "She dragged Alex out there one morning, and he moaned about having to go."

"Maybe it's one of those tedious aeroplane museums," Helen said. "All those hunks of junk lying around for people to ogle at. I can't imagine anything more boring."

I sat up in my seat. "Maybe it's more than that. What if you can learn to fly there?"

Helen stopped the car outside the house and turned to look at me. "Do you think Piers and Harriet have been taking private lessons at this place?"

"They could have learned to fly a drone there."

"I doubt an aeroplane museum would offer lessons in how to fly an armed drone."

"They wouldn't need to learn how to fly an *armed* drone," I said. "All they'd need to do was get good at flying a model plane or a normal drone. That would give them the skills they'd need."

"I'm not sure." Helen opened the car door and climbed out. I followed her with Flipper. "Neither Piers nor Harriet strike me as the kind of people who'd be interested in learning how to fly a model plane."

"They would if they had an ulterior motive."

"What about Eva's theory about Alex?" Helen walked to the front door. "He definitely knows how to do it."

"So Eva says," I said. "But Mickey Kill wasn't complimentary about her. He said not to trust her."

"Since when have we started trusting anything Mickey Kill has to say?" Helen asked. "And, why would Eva want her brother jailed for a murder he didn't commit?"

I sighed as I followed Helen to the kitchen. "I'm not sure. Maybe they secretly hate each other. Or she's jealous of him and wants to be the center of attention. Do you remember when we first arrived, and Camilla didn't even mention Eva? That sort of benign neglect must sting."

As we entered the kitchen, the temperature was much cooler. Greg was drifting around the table, a sad look on his face.

Helen rubbed her hands together. "Have we got company?"

Flipper ran to where Greg was floating and sat at his feet.

"We have." I placed the cakes on the table and took off my jacket. "I don't suppose you want to help us whittle down some of these suspects we're puzzling over?"

Greg looked up at me and shrugged.

"Just a few hints would help," I said. "Was it a man or a woman?"

Greg pointed out the window.

"Of course, it was night time." I let out another sigh. "You wouldn't have seen who shot you."

"Especially not if he was running away from a drone," Helen said. "If it had been me, I'd have sprinted like an Olympic athlete."

Greg nodded and continued floating around the kitchen table, Flipper following at his heel.

"And you're certain Alex didn't kill you?" I said to him.

Greg pulled up short and shook his head violently.

"What does he think of that?" Helen asked.

"He's still not keen on Alex being the killer."

Greg shook the table, the legs bouncing up and down.

Flipper hurried over and looked hopefully at the bag of cakes that wobbled on the edge.

I grabbed the cakes and shoved them away from Flipper's waiting mouth. "Calm down," I said to Greg. "We're trying to figure out who hurt you. We learned tonight that Piers stole a business from you."

The table stopped shaking. Greg gave me a puzzled look.

"It was your new dating app."

The same puzzled look remained on his face.

"Does he think it was them?" Helen asked.

"Greg just looks confused." I took a deep breath. I'd never met such an uncertain ghost before. "Did Piers steal your app?"

Greg shrugged. His image faded, and his gaze went to the floor.

It looked as if he had given up the fight, almost as if he didn't care what had happened to him. If that was the case, why was he still here?

"We need to find the evidence for ourselves," Helen said.

"It looks like we'll have to." I watched as Greg slowly faded away. I wished he had a bit more backbone, but I felt sorry for him. He seemed so sad and lonely.

Maybe he'd been unhappy when he was alive as well. People like Piers and Harriet preyed on vulnerable eccentrics like Greg and Alex. It wasn't fair. It made me all the more determined to help him.

Chapter 17

"That's a no to the party at the Ritz in London. A no to the opening of the new art gallery in Winchester, and you definitely don't want to go to the paint balling millionaires' activity day in Hampshire?" I'd finally made my way through all the invitations Alex had received over the last three months. Every one he'd turned down.

Alex glanced up from his usual position on the couch. "That's right. Parties exhaust me. I've never really understood art, and can you see me with a paint gun in my hand, running through a forest with a bunch of egomaniacs?"

He had a point, although he was handy with a gun when it had anything to do with his computer games, and possibly when it came to flying armed drones and killing his best friend.

After my conversations with Eva and Mickey Kill, I was on the fence as to who had harmed Greg. Alex had the means to do it, but I wasn't sure of his motives. Harriet and Piers would gain from Greg being out of the way, but from what I knew, neither of them had any clue about armed drones. Add to that Greg's confusion about whether Piers actually stole anything from him, and I'd gotten no closer to the truth.

I looked at the final invitation sitting on the desk, an open day at the local airbase. It came complete with a funfair, food, and drink, and the opportunity to fly your own drone.

"Here's one that's local." I lifted the plain green invitation. "It's an air show at the base this weekend. That would be easy to get to."

Alex shook his head. "Mom makes me spend far too much time there as it is. I don't want to go dragging around there at the weekend, especially not when it'll be full of people staring at all the aircraft."

"They invited you as a special guest to open the event," I said. "They must want a local celebrity."

"Then they've got the wrong person," Alex said. "I've never been into ribbon cutting ceremonies."

"It could be fun," I said. "I might go."

"I wouldn't waste your time," he said. "Unless you're into boring planes like Mom is."

"I take it you're not into planes?"

He shrugged. "Not really. Unless they're part of a computer simulation."

"Maybe you can attend with Piers and Harriet."

Alex laughed. "Is there free champagne on offer?"

I scanned the invitation. "I'm sure the organizers would look after you."

"Harriet doesn't go anywhere unless there's free champagne. I guess Piers might be up for tagging along, though. It depends what's in it for him."

"He's not into model aircraft?"

"He's into models of the female kind, but nothing to do with planes." Alex glanced over. "Why do you want them there?"

"I wanted to see if I could tempt you along if your friends came." In truth, if I could get Alex to the air show with the others, I could use it as an opportunity to see how much Harriet and Piers knew about drones.

I checked the contact information. "I'll suggest someone else open the event."

"If you like," Alex said.

I whisked off a quick email to the organizer, suggesting local socialite Harriet Fawcett would be delighted to open the event on behalf of Alex.

The reply was almost instant and full of enthusiasm. They would be thrilled to have Harriet attend in Alex's place and happy she could be their special guest for the day. They sent through information about the event and what Harriet needed to do—simply say a thank you to everyone for coming along and cut the ribbon to mark the official start of the event.

It sounded simple enough. I just had to convince Harriet to turn up on the day and reveal herself as one of Greg's killers.

"I've suggested Harriet open the air show," I said to Alex. "Do you think she'd like to be the center of attention?"

He shrugged. "She'd love that. But I can't see Harriet in a muddy field. It would ruin her high heels."

"I can get her a pair of welly boots. They do them in all different colors. Do you think she'd like ones with glitter?"

"I don't dare comment on anything Harriet wears," Alex said. "I once said her dress was pretty, and she tore it up! I thought women liked compliments."

"Normally, we do." Harriet's temper tantrums were another tick in the suspect box. Maybe Greg had said the wrong thing to her, and she'd lost control.

"I've never figured out how her mind works," Alex said. "She might like to do it. She might also like glittery wellies. Equally, she might hate the idea and get stroppy and refuse to speak to anyone for a week."

"It'll keep her occupied for the day, which means you can do whatever you like."

Alex paused his game and looked at me. "That's not such a bad idea. What will she need to do?"

"Hob nob with the local mayor and other dignitaries," I said. "Give a short opening speech and cut the official ribbon. Then she can enjoy herself. If there's no champagne provided, I can bring a bottle for her."

Alex tugged on his bottom lip. "If she's busy doing that, I can stay here without her complaining about the time I spend on my games."

"You might need to come along for a little while to make sure she's happy," I said. "It will be easy enough for you to slip away while Harriet's occupied. What do you reckon?"

"Go for it," Alex said. "Harriet's been getting demanding lately. She keeps dropping hints about moving in."

"You don't want that?"

"I'm too young to have a serious girlfriend," Alex said, "and far too young to be moving in with one."

"Have you told her that?"

"Have you met Harriet?"

Unfortunately, I had. "Maybe she'll find someone else who's ready to get serious with her." Someone like Piers, for example.

"I sort of hope she does that soon," Alex said. "I don't mind having fun with her, but I never wanted it to get serious. Harriet isn't great at taking a hint. She used to get in the way when Greg was around and slow down our progress with work. She intimidated the heck out of him. Greg used to hide in the kitchen when she was being particularly spiteful."

"She didn't like Greg?"

"I'm not sure Harriet likes anyone. She's even mean to Lucy." Alex looked over to where Lucy was fast asleep on her favorite pillow in the corner of the room. Flipper was lying next to her. And next to him was Priscilla, who'd decided she liked the house a lot more than the outbuilding.

"How can anybody not like Lucy?"

"Exactly. I need a girlfriend who doesn't mind me having a pet pig and lets me play on these games for hours. Someone who joined in would be even better." Alex glanced at me. "Someone like you, just younger."

I tried not to be offended. "Maybe you could play a little less. I know you do it in the name of your research, but sometimes, real life can be just as entertaining."

Alex wrinkled his nose. "You can keep real life. I'm happy here." His shoulders slumped, and he stared at the controller in his hand.

Alex wasn't happy. Maybe he had been when Greg was around and there was someone who understood him. But for all the material wealth around him, he was lonely, just like Greg.

No matter the evidence against Alex, I couldn't figure him for killing Greg and taking away the only person who understood him.

"How about some lunch?" I asked.

Flipper, Priscilla, and Lucy lifted their heads, and three tails wagged.

"Will Helen be too unhappy if I order instant noodles again?" Alex asked.

"She'll make you whatever you like," I said. "But she is a great cook. You should let her make you something from scratch."

"The pizza she made me was good," Alex said. "I enjoyed that. And she did homemade garlic bread to go alongside it. That was great."

"She can make you Thai food," I said. "She's amazing at that."

"Maybe Helen can flavor the instant noodles so they taste like Thai food," Alex said.

"I'll suggest that to her." I sighed as I left the room, Flipper, Priscilla, and Lucy following me to the kitchen. It was a start, but Alex was into his instant noodles, and there was nothing I could do to change that.

Helen sat at the kitchen table. She had several cookery books open and was scribbling notes on a notepad.

"I'm here with the lunchtime order," I said.

Helen's expression soured. "Let me guess, fish finger sandwiches with mayonnaise? Or does he want tomato sauce this time with a side order of ready salted chips?"

"No, something far fancier than that."

Her expression brightened. "What does he want?"

"Thai flavored instant noodles."

Helen pressed her lips together and then nodded. "That will take me all of five minutes to prepare. I bet he doesn't want any vegetables either."

I sat at the table. "Vegetables weren't mentioned. But you have four hungry mouths here who are willing to eat your great food."

Helen looked at Flipper and the pigs. "They're not eating my cooking. But I can make us a nice meal. I've got plenty of time on my hands. Instant noodles and grilling fish fingers don't exactly occupy my time."

"What about Camilla and Eva?" I asked. "They must want something different."

"Eva lives off cereal she eats from the packet. Camilla's not around all that much," Helen said. "When she is, she only wants plain things. I don't think she even notices what she's eating."

"I always love your food," I said. "And Flipper is always happy to eat any leftovers. It looks like Lucy and Priscilla will be too."

Flipper, Lucy, and Priscilla sat patiently by the kitchen table, watching Helen's every move. They knew she was an excellent source of tasty treats.

"I'm not sure I can get references from a dog and two pigs," Helen said. "I don't think they'll stand me in good stead for getting another job."

A thread of worry traced through me. "You don't want to stay here?"

Helen opened a packet of noodles and dumped them into a bowl before pouring hot water over them. "Not if this is all I get to do. I'm bored."

"And maybe missing Gunner?"

She stirred the noodles with a wooden spoon, her back to me. "A little bit. I didn't think I would miss him. He can be so annoying and loud. But I sort of like that."

"He'll be here at the weekend," I said. "And I have a plan for when Gunner and Zach arrive. We're going to take them to an air show."

"There's an air show nearby?"

"Yes. And I've arranged for Harriet to be the guest of honor. They're having drone demonstrations all day. Visitors can try their hand at flying their own drone."

Helen pulled the noodles out of the water and mixed in lemongrass and fish sauce. "How are you going to get Harriet to fly a drone?"

"I'm hoping that she'll have to try everything as the special guest. We just need to watch to see how good she is."

"What about Piers?"

"I bet he'll be there too. Piers is never far behind Harriet. And I've persuaded Alex to put in an appearance. That'll give Piers another reason to tag along and play at being best buddies with him."

Helen dumped the noodles on a plate. "I feel sorry for Alex. For all this money, he doesn't have much of a life or any friends."

"I was thinking exactly the same," I said. "Now Greg has gone, he's all alone. He can't have harmed him."

"I really hope it was Harriet and Piers," Helen said. "Although, prison food would suit Alex. I imagine they serve a lot of fish fingers and instant noodles behind bars." She hurried out of the kitchen with the noodles on a plate.

I sent a quick text message to Zach, letting him know what we'd be getting up to at the weekend. It wasn't the most romantic way to spend a weekend, hunting a killer at an air show, but he always said he wanted to keep me safe when I was helping a ghost. This would be the perfect opportunity for him to do that.

I got back an instant reply. *I'll bring my aviator sunglasses and flying jacket.*

I had to smile. He would look good in aviator sunglasses. Zach looked good in just about anything.

When he got here, and we finally figured out what had happened to Greg, I'd spend time alone with him and figure out our own ghostly problem.

Chapter 18

I waved as I saw Zach's Land Rover approach the house.

It was the day of the air show, and I couldn't help but feel nervously excited. It wasn't just that we'd hopefully uncover what had happened to Greg, but I'd missed Zach and was worried about him. I hated the thought that he was in our house with Amelia, and she was causing problems between us.

Flipper ran up to the Land Rover as it stopped. A second later, Jessie shot out. They danced around each other, happy to be reunited.

Lucy and Priscilla stood a few steps behind Flipper, watching the two dogs.

Helen ran out the front door of the house and flung herself at Gunner as he emerged from the Land Rover, almost knocking him over.

He gave a startled laugh before wrapping his arms around her and spinning her in a circle.

Zach got out and smiled at me. Our greeting was more cautious. We were tiptoeing around each other, both knowing there was a problem and not sure how to solve it.

He kissed my cheek. "It's good to see you."

"You too." He smelled of his usual combination of spicy cologne and grass. I had missed that smell.

"So, an air show," Zach said. "I didn't think this was your thing."

"It's not," I said. "I have an ulterior motive."

Helen led Gunner over, their hands clasped together.

Gunner slowed and peered over my shoulder. "What are those pigs doing here?"

"That's Lucy and Priscilla," I said. "They're Flipper's new friends. They're nice pigs."

We all watched as Lucy and Priscilla trotted over to Flipper and Jessie. Jessie stared at them for a few seconds, confusion clear on her doggy face.

After a few mutual sniffs and touching of noses, Jessie seemed to accept Lucy and Priscilla, and they ran across the lawn together.

"If only human relationships were that easy to figure out," Helen said. "A few sniffs in the right place, and everything works out."

"What's your ulterior motive for going to this air show?" Zach asked.

"We're going to catch a killer," Helen said.

"Babe, are you sure about that? That sounds dangerous," Gunner said.

"We'll be fine. This isn't the first time we've caught a killer." She booped him on the end of the nose with her finger.

"You already know the basics," I said. "Our prime suspects will be at this air show. They're having drone flying at the event. It's a chance for us to see them in action."

"These possible killers are hardly going to re-enact their crime," Gunner said.

"No, but if we can see that they know how to fly a drone, it'll be more evidence against them."

"Give me everything you have on these potential killers. I'll make a few discreet calls before we go to the air show," Gunner said. "We need to know who we're dealing with."

"I don't want you putting yourself at any risk." Helen clutched Gunner's hand.

"Sweetheart, that's sort of my job." He winked at Helen.

I gave him everything I knew about Harriet and Piers.

Gunner ambled off, his phone glued to his ear. Helen was close behind him, obviously listening in to his call.

Suddenly, I felt awkward being alone with Zach. "So, how are things?"

Zach's forehead wrinkled. "The business is good. I've got two more jobs on the books this week."

"That's great."

He gently took hold of my hand. "Things are still going missing."

My heart sank. "Amelia is still around?"

"I think so. She's not causing much of a problem. I just wish she'd stop hiding my stuff."

"You still have no idea why she's hanging around you?"

"I thought maybe it was because I still had some of her things," Zach said. "You know, you keep things for sentimental reasons. I moved them, and even asked her if that was the problem, but nothing's changed."

"You do keep things if you care about someone," I said. "Do you still care about Amelia?"

"Lorna, it's not like that. We were together for a while," Zach said.

My throat felt tight. "So, you do still care?"

"Not in the way I care about you," he said. "She's a part of my past, though. I can't erase that, even if I want to."

"What do you have of Amelia's?"

"That's just it, nothing anymore. I went through all the final boxes of things I hadn't unpacked. The only thing I've got left is the ring and a few old pictures."

"Maybe that's it," I said. "Amelia wants you to do something with her wedding ring."

"I left it out thinking she might take it, but it hasn't moved. If it was the ring, don't you think she'd have taken it?"

"Most likely," I said. "I wish she'd show us what she wants, instead of hiding. Amelia must know I'm not happy with her being there."

"She was never shy about telling me what she wanted," Zach said. "She could be a bit spiteful. That could be the whole reason she's doing this."

"You think she's jealous of your happiness?"

"That's a distinct possibility," Zach said. "We didn't part as friends, not after she cheated on me."

"Maybe that's it," I said. "Amelia wants you to be friends. She could be feeling bad about how things ended between you and wants to say sorry."

"She can say sorry by leaving us alone," Zach said. "She didn't have to turn up and move things. That's only causing us problems."

As much as I hated to admit it, he was right. I gave his hand a gentle squeeze. "We'll figure this out. We're not going to let a ghost come between us, are we?"

"Not for a second." He kissed my forehead.

"I've got nothing on this Harriet or Piers." Gunner strolled back, Helen by his side. "Piers has a few unpaid speeding tickets, but nothing serious. Harriet has no record."

"It doesn't mean they're innocent, though," I said. "It simply means they haven't been caught."

"Excellent deduction, Watson," Gunner said. "Let's head over to this air show and see if we can find out if they committed the crime."

"Wait just a second," I said. "I need to make sure Alex is awake before we leave, or he'll miss the whole thing."

Zach looked at his watch. "Your boss is still in bed? It's almost noon."

"He's a night owl," I said. "He spends his evenings online, gaming with people in America."

"Is your boss a teenage boy?" Gunner asked.

"Most of the time he acts like one." I hurried back to the house. "I won't be a minute." As I entered the lounge, I discovered Alex just waking up on the couch.

He gave me a sleepy smile and ran a hand through his messy hair. "Is it time for breakfast?"

"It's time you got up and got yourself ready," I said. "The air show starts in less than an hour."

"I don't want to go," he grumbled. "I'm... sick."

"You're fine," I said. "Have some coffee and something to eat. You'll enjoy it when you get there."

"You sound just like Greg," Alex said. "He always used to say the same thing."

"Was he right?"

"Sometimes, but it was always more fun when he was around." Alex slumped back on the couch and covered his face with an arm.

"You know, you will have other friends." I sat on the edge of the couch. "I know you must miss Greg a lot, but maybe it's time you found someone else to get involved in your business. Someone who understands you and works well with you."

"Please don't suggest Piers."

I laughed. "I definitely don't think you should go into business with Piers. In fact, I'm not sure he's that good of an influence on you."

"Now you sound like my mom." Alex pulled himself into a sitting position. "She can't stand Piers. She's not keen on Harriet either."

"Then your mom is a good judge of character," I said. "What did she think about Greg?"

Alex scratched a hand through his hair again. "Not that much, actually. She always said I could do better. She said he held me back. I never listened to her. She doesn't know the first thing about gaming. Greg, on the other hand, was wired for computers. I used to joke with him that he had a circuit board for a brain."

"How about setting up in business with Mickey Kill? He knows his way around games."

The computer screen flashed up a skull and cross bones and a booing sound echoed through the speakers.

Alex chuckled. "He doesn't like that idea."

"Do you know that Mickey Kill listens in to what's going on here?"

"Of course I do," Alex said. "I let him. I gave him access to the webcams ages ago."

"Isn't that a bit risky? He can see everything you do."

"Mickey Kill lives by the gamers' code. Greg trusted him, so do I."

"But not as a business partner?"

"It's not his sort of thing," Alex said. "He's a great gamer. We all have our own specialities. His isn't business."

"Fair enough. But I know one thing for sure; you'll never find any new friends if you spend your life on this couch. I know it's not comfortable getting out there and meeting new people, but you need to do it. Coming to this air show today will be a first step."

"I'm hardly going to find a new best friend at the air show."

"Maybe not. But it'll give you practice. You never know. You could meet some nice people there." Or some truly horrible ones, the people who killed his best friend and left him lonely and unhappy.

"I can drop by for ten minutes."

I heard a car horn and jumped to my feet. "Promise me you'll come?"

Alex sighed. "I'll be there."

I wasn't convinced. "Promise me on your gamers' code."

Alex grimaced. "You have no idea what the gamers' code is, do you?"

"I've played more computer games in the last week than I have in the last decade," I said. "Of course I have no clue what the gamers' code is."

Alex grinned. "Fair enough. On the gamers' code, I'll be there."

"I'll see you later." I hurried back to the Land Rover, where Helen was leaning over to press the horn again.

"I'm here." I jumped in the back and sat next to Jessie and Flipper.

"What took you so long?" Helen asked.

"I was checking in on Alex," I said. "He's a bit down. He wasn't sure he was coming to the air show."

"Helen has been filling us in on the other suspects," Gunner said. "Alex is one of them."

"I don't think he is," I said. "He's too much of a nice guy."

"Nice guys can snap," Gunner said. "I've seen it happen."

"Not this one," I said. "We need to keep focused on Harriet and Piers."

"Alex's fake best friend and the horrible girlfriend," Gunner said.

Helen had been doing a good job of filling them in. "That's right. Harriet is the guest of honor today. I'm sure Piers will show up at some point."

"What about this sister?" Zach asked as he drove us along the narrow lane and out onto the main road heading toward the air show. "Helen mentioned she might be involved."

"I thought that at first," I said. "She's keen on pointing her finger at her brother. Maybe she's deflecting her involvement by focusing on him."

"Will she be there today?" Zach asked.

"Most likely," I said.

"Point the suspects out when we get there," Gunner said. "We can keep tabs on them."

The traffic increased as we got near to the air show. We joined a slow-moving queue of cars to enter the airfield.

"I did a bit of investigating into this place before we arrived," Gunner said. "It's mainly military aircraft here."

I sat up straight. "I thought this was a dusty old museum for defunct planes?"

"There's nothing dusty about this place," Gunner said. "If you listen to the rumors, they do interesting testing here."

"What do they test?" Helen asked.

"State-of-the-art military craft," Gunner said. "Stealth planes, new types of propulsion systems. Unmanned aircraft."

"Including armed drones?" I asked.

"Including armed drones," Gunner said.

"This must be the place Alex worked when he took on a contract with the military," I said.

"Why are they opening today if the public isn't supposed to get a look at this kind of thing?" Helen asked.

"To show they're honest and not up to anything nefarious," Gunner said. "They'll keep the top-secret stuff out of sight. My contact in the local force gave me a summary of the case findings. Greg's body was found in the field next to the airbase. He was shot in the back, which suggests he was trying to get away."

That tallied with everything Greg had told us.

We stop talking as we reached the entrance gate and passed through. As we rounded the corner, I saw a dozen aircraft lined up on an airstrip and a huge open hangar with more aircraft inside.

The place was already busy with families looking forward to a fun day trip. Carnival music filled the air, and the scent of hot sugar drifted through the open window. But I wasn't in the mood to eat. I was in the mood to figure out who'd killed Greg.

We all climbed out of the Land Rover and headed toward the hangar.

"Oh no," Helen muttered. "I've just spotted Harriet."

I looked over to where Helen pointed. Harriet was wearing a fitted cream dress with matching jacket. She was tottering along on high black heels, her hair curled around her face. She was on the arm of a middle-aged man in a suit, who was pointing things out to her.

"Keep an eye on her," I said. "She'll not be going too far in those heels."

"And there's Piers," Helen said.

Piers trailed along behind Harriet, a glass of beer in his hand. He looked distinctly bored and not at all amused to be there.

"At least they're together," I said. "It'll be easier to keep track of them."

"It doesn't look like we'll need to do that," Helen said. "We've been spotted."

Harriet left the man in the suit and stalked toward me, a scowl on her face. "Where is he?"

"Good morning to you, too," I said.

Harriet waved a hand in front of her face. "Alex. I thought you'd be bringing him with you."

"He's on his way."

"You're supposed to be his assistant."

I smiled serenely. "That's right."

"You should assist him to get here on time," Harriet said. "I've been forced to look at far too many tedious aeroplanes. Alex should be here to keep me entertained."

"Haven't you got Piers to do that?" Helen asked sweetly.

Harriet glanced over her shoulder, and her cheeks reddened. "He's just... a friend."

"A friend with benefits," Helen muttered.

The sound of buzzing had me looking skyward. It was a drone flying overhead. "Have you had a go on that?" I pointed at the drone.

Harriet shrugged. "That's not my thing. Actually, none of this is my thing. I'm doing it because Alex said I'd be representing him. He'll be impressed by me being here in his name. It makes us official. I'm practically his wife if he wants me to do this sort of thing!"

"Not quite," Helen said.

"You should try everything here," I said. "It's only right, you being the guest of honor."

"The stupid organizer has been trying to get me to take part." Harriet looked over her shoulder at the man in the suit. "He seems to think I'm interested in this."

I suppressed a smile. I had played up Harriet's interest in aircraft when I'd suggested her as the guest of honor. "You should still give it a try. There could be some good photo opportunities in it for you."

She paused and looked around. "I haven't been able to take any photos. I lost my phone."

I inhaled sharply and pressed my lips together. It was still hiding in my bedroom. "When did you last see it?"

Harriet's brow wrinkled. "Actually, at Alex's. Have you seen it?"

"No. But I'll keep an eye out for it."

"Alex was always telling me I should put a tracker on it so I could find it if this ever happened." Harriet shrugged. "Not that it matters. It's time for an upgrade, anyway."

I let out a gentle sigh. "So, how about the drones?"

"I already told you I'm not interested." Harriet scowled at me. "Make sure you come find me as soon as Alex arrives. He needs to be by my side on this important day. People need to see us together."

She stalked away, and I shook my head.

"She's a charmer," Gunner said.

"You're seeing her good side," I said.

"She isn't keen on trying out the drones," Zach said. "She could be hiding something."

"Either that or she doesn't want to make herself look like an idiot," Helen said.

"Too late for that," Gunner said. "That girl has a serious lack of appeal."

"You think so?" Helen grinned at him. "She's quite pretty."

Gunner wrapped an arm around her waist. "She pales into insignificance compared to you."

Helen giggled. "Shall we get candy floss?"

"No candy floss," I said. "We need to keep focused on the suspects."

"We can see Harriet and Piers from here," Gunner said.

"And Alex isn't here yet," Helen said.

"What about Eva?" I looked around, but there were so many people, it was hard to pick anyone out in the crowd.

"I'll look out for a pale woman in black while we get the candy floss." Helen was, already dragging Gunner away.

"A woman in black?" Zach asked.

"Eva is in mourning for Greg," I said. "She had a bit of a crush on him."

"What about the ghost?" Zach asked. "Has he put in an appearance today?"

"He rarely does," I said. "He's introverted. Every time we see him, he just seems sad. He doesn't know who killed him, but he's convinced it wasn't Alex."

"As are you," Zach said.

"I can't figure him for a killer," I said. "You haven't met him yet, but I know you'll like him when you do."

"I won't like him if he killed his best friend," Zach said. "I also won't like him if he's put you at any risk."

I loved it when Zach got all protective of me. "He hasn't. Alex is a decent guy."

Helen returned with four sticks of pink candy floss. "We might as well enjoy ourselves while we're here. We can hunt for our killers and eat this at the same time."

I took the enormous puffy cloud of pink sugar and took a bite. I got an instant sugar rush, and my teeth ached.

"Isn't that Camilla?" Helen asked through a mouthful of candy floss.

Camilla strode toward us. She wore a green jumpsuit and carried a helmet under one arm.

"What's she doing dressed like that?" I asked.

"Didn't you say she volunteers here?" Helen said. "Maybe it's part of her volunteer duties."

"I thought she helped in the aeroplane museum, not on this actual base," I said.

"You won't have regular volunteers on military airbases like this," Gunner said. "It's all skilled personnel at a place like this. Volunteers would be too much of a risk."

"Maybe this one is different," Helen said.

I lowered my candy floss. Maybe it wasn't. If Camilla had easy access to this site, could she get her hands on a drone?

She raised a hand in greeting. "I'm so glad to see you here. What do you think of our little air show?"

"We wouldn't miss it." I introduced her to Gunner and Zach. "What's the outfit for?"

"Oh, this," Camilla said. "I always wear it when I go flying. It's standard issue."

"I didn't know you flew," I said.

"That's what I do," Camilla said. "I've got my own small plane here. I love going out on a sunny day like this. I'm taking people up on flights today."

"That must be fun." Helen was too high on sugar to notice the connection.

Was this all a coincidence? Camilla could handle a plane and knew her way around this airbase. But why would she want her son's best friend dead?

"It's lots of fun," Camilla said. "Do you both fancy getting sky bound?"

I stared at her, and gulped. "Get in an actual plane with you?"

She chuckled. "Of course. I have plenty of experience. Come on. Take a risk. I promise, I won't crash."

Helen nodded enthusiastically. "Why not?"

I wasn't so sure. Camilla might not crash the plane, but what if she was the killer?

Chapter 19

"I'll be busy for the rest of the day, so you may as well get in before the crowds line up," Camilla said. "I'm doing three flights an hour. Since the event isn't officially open yet, you get the first chance to get on the plane with me."

I did want to know more about Camilla's involvement at the airbase but wasn't sure about doing it while she flew us through the clouds. "We don't want to stop other people from enjoying themselves."

"Nonsense. I insist." Camilla tapped the top of her helmet. "You can call it a perk of the job."

"Come on. It'll be brilliant." Helen gave me a curious look, finally seeming to realize that something was wrong.

I wanted to tell her my concerns, but there was no way of doing so without alerting Camilla.

"Hold on a moment. There's Alex." Camilla hurried past us before I could think of another excuse not to get on the plane. She grabbed hold of him and yanked him toward us. "You're late."

"I got here as soon as I could," Alex said. He looked at the group and nodded at everyone.

"You haven't even showered," Camilla said. "What have you done to your hair?" She tried to smooth down his messy hair.

"Mom, I'm fine." Alex stepped out of her reach. "I said I'd come." He looked at me and shrugged.

"It's good to see you here," I said. "Your mom was just offering to take us on a flight."

"Sure, she does that," Alex said.

"We didn't even know Camilla flew," Helen said. "Lorna's too scared to go on the plane in case it crashes."

"It's not that! I'm sure you're a great pilot." I looked at Camilla.

"I'm excellent," she said.

"Mom was one of the first female pilots in the RAF," Alex said.

"You're kidding," Helen said. "You must be really good."

"I've flown hundreds of missions," Camilla said.

"Mom is good at what she does," Alex said. "She's been trying to convince me to get my pilot's license, but I prefer the type of flying where I don't need to leave the couch."

I smiled at him. There was no surprise there.

"Let's go, you two," Camilla said. "I don't have much time. We must keep to the schedule."

I looked at Helen, who was bouncing on her toes with excitement. My gut told me it was a huge mistake to get on this plane, but I needed to know more.

"Let's do it," Helen said. "It will be fun."

Forcing down my concerns, I nodded.

"I'll keep an eye on Flipper for you," Zach said.

Flipper was happily sniffing the ground with Jessie by his side. I had no concerns about him.

I leaned over to Zach. "Make sure you don't let Harriet or Piers out of your sight." I still had them in my firing line, but this new information about Camilla had muddled my thoughts.

"You can count on me," he whispered and kissed my cheek.

I hurried along behind Camilla with Helen, leaving Zach and Gunner to get acquainted with Alex.

"This is mine," Camilla said, as we stopped by a small white plane with red piping down the side. "It's a Cessna TTx. I've had her for two years. She can go almost thirteen hundred nautical miles."

I inspected the plane. It looked safe enough. As for the pilot, I wasn't so sure.

Camilla handed us both helmets. "You need these so we can talk to each other when we're inside. It gets noisy."

Helen reluctantly put on the helmet. "This will ruin my hair. I spent ages getting my curls just right this morning."

"Gunner will still love you, even when you have helmet hair," I said.

Camilla climbed into the front of the plane, and we followed her. I took the seat right behind Camilla, and Helen took the one in the back.

"Can you hear me okay?" Camilla said through the helmet audio.

"Loud and clear," I said.

"Me too," Helen said. "Are you any good at doing tricks?"

Camilla laughed. "If you want tricks, I can show you plenty of those. It's why I'm doing this today. The organizers want to give the crowd something to remember." She ran through a few flight checks before starting the engine.

My stomach gave a nervous lurch. "Don't do anything too dramatic."

"We might as well have fun while we're here," Helen said. "How many chances are we going to get to be flown by a former RAF pilot?"

"Quite right." Camilla taxied the plane onto the runway.

I took a deep breath. There was no going back now. It would be fine. I wouldn't be at all scared, and I needed time to process this new information about Camilla. Maybe I was getting it wrong. Just because she could fly an actual plane, it didn't mean she had anything to do with drones. Even if she did, why would she want Greg dead?

The plane's engine roared as we picked up speed. The take-off was perfect, and we were soon in the air, zooming above the crowds.

Camilla did a circuit of the village, staying low so we got a good view. "That's our house down there to the left, the one with the circular lawn out front."

I looked down and saw the house.

"You can see the church to your right and the woods just behind it." We did a complete loop before Camilla took us higher.

"Do you ever get Alex and Eva flying?" I asked.

"Not often. Eva's too busy skulking around her room and moping about nothing in particular. Alex, as you have seen, enjoys his couch a little too much."

"I can't believe they don't enjoy this," Helen said. "You can see for miles."

"I only ever got Alex in here when Greg was around," Camilla said.

"Greg liked to fly?" I asked.

Camilla was quiet for a few seconds. "He did."

"I think Alex misses him."

"I can't imagine why," Camilla said swiftly. "They were so competitive with each other."

"They were best friends, though, weren't they?" I asked

"How do you know that?"

"Alex talks about Greg. I think he's lonely."

"That boy needs to get out more," Camilla said. "He can do better than Greg. He was holding him back."

"Why do you think that?"

There was more silence from Camilla. "A mother always knows best. Now for some fun." The plane banked sharply right.

I held in a scream as the plane flipped over.

Helen squealed with delight and clapped her hands together. "Do it again."

"Once was enough," I gasped.

Camilla laughed and repeated the trick.

My breakfast was definitely not happy with these flips.

"Can you do a dive?" Helen asked.

"No! No dives!" I said.

"Of course I can dive," Camilla said. "We were trained to get out of dangerous situations when I flew RAF jets. Diving is a great way to get the enemy off your tail. Some aircraft can't go below a certain altitude. It's also a good way to extinguish a fire in the engine."

"We're not on fire, though." I checked the engine. No fire, so no diving.

"Let's try a dive," Helen said.

"Hold onto your hats, ladies." Camilla swooped the plane toward the ground.

I squeezed my eyes shut and gripped the sides of my seat. We were going to die. I just knew it.

"This is amazing," Helen yelled. "I can see the people below us."

I risked a peek before shutting my eyes again. "We're too close to the ground!" How on earth were we going to survive this?

"Don't you trust me?" Camilla asked, her voice high with excitement.

I wasn't sure I did trust Camilla. Not anymore. I felt my stomach lift as the plane shot back into the sky.

"You're so clever," Helen said. "No wonder you were in the RAF."

I moistened my teeth with my tongue and risked opening my eyes. I let out a sigh. The plane was level again, and we were still alive.

"I can handle any aircraft," Camilla said. "A few years ago, a commercial airline tried to sweet talk me into ferrying hyperactive holidaymakers to and from the Continent. Despite the enticing salary, I declined. There's no challenge in flying airbuses. I love this kind of plane, though. They add a bit of spice to life. You have to be totally focused. Keeping my girl in the air requires precision and skill."

I took a few deep breaths and forced myself to stop panicking. My gaze settled on the back of Camilla's head. "I don't suppose you know how to fly drones?"

"Of course! Like I said, I can fly anything."

A horrible sense of dread slid over me. "You'll have to show me how to fly one once we get back on the ground. They look like fun."

"If you're into that sort of thing," Camilla said. "They're child's play compared to a real plane. I can fly one in my sleep."

Suddenly, I wanted out of this plane.

Chapter 20

My heart still raced as the plane touched down. I scrambled out of the seat and pulled off my helmet. I needed to get my thoughts in order. Could Camilla have killed Greg? Alex said she didn't think much of him, and she could fly a drone. But I still couldn't work out why she'd want him dead.

"Are you okay?" Helen caught hold of my elbow. "You're looking a little green."

Camilla strolled over and took the helmets from us. "Any time you want another flight, just let me know. I'm often over here. I'm always happy to take people up in the air."

"Thanks," I croaked out. "I'll check my diary. I'm going to be busy for the next few years."

Camilla laughed. "Not all of us are meant for adventures in the sky. Maybe you're better on terra firma, keeping an eye on Alex."

"You could be right," I said.

"It's almost time for the air show to open," Camilla said. "I'll see you at the ribbon cutting." She walked back to the plane, leaving me alone with Helen.

"Are you sure you're okay?" Helen asked. "You really don't look well."

"It's not the flight that's the problem," I said. "Did you hear what Camilla had to say about flying drones?"

"It doesn't surprise me that she can pilot one," Helen said. "She's an ace in the sky. And she was in the RAF. How glamorous."

"There's nothing glamorous about it if she was the one who piloted the drone that killed Greg."

Helen's mouth fell open. "What about Harriet and Piers? We're sure it's them, aren't we?"

"Not anymore." I glanced over my shoulder to make sure Camilla was out of earshot.

"Why would Camilla kill Greg?"

"She can be controlling, especially with Alex. Maybe Greg said or did something to Alex, and Camilla didn't like it."

"I'm still hedging my bets that it's Harriet and Piers," Helen said. "I get Camilla is protective of her son, but she wouldn't kill his best friend."

I groaned. Maybe all the diving and flipping was getting my thoughts jumbled. "You could be right. Let's go find Zach and Gunner, see what Harriet's been up to while we've been in the air." My knees had finally stopped shaking as we walked through the crowds.

"There's Gunner!" Helen bounded ahead of me, waving her hand over her head. She had an inability to hide the fact she was seriously smitten with him.

My eyes narrowed as I saw Zach had company. Harriet was standing far too close to him for my liking, one hand on his bicep. As I got closer, she gave a false sounding laugh and step even nearer to my man.

Zach glanced up as I arrived and gave me a pleading look. "How was your flight?" He deliberately stepped away from Harriet.

"Scary," I said.

Harriet narrowed the gap between her and Zach. "Perhaps we can take a flight together some time."

"I wonder what Alex will think about that." I stared daggers at Harriet.

"He won't care," Harriet said. "He'll be too busy making his next million for me to spend."

I snorted a laugh. If Alex had his way, Harriet wouldn't be there for much longer to spend all his money. Pushing aside my jealousy, I smiled sweetly at Harriet. "Have you had a chance to fly the drones yet?"

Harriet sighed. "Why are you so obsessed with those stupid drones?"

"I'm not. But it's important to try everything."

"I'd rather not."

"You are the event's guest of honor," I said. "It will look rude if you don't take part."

"Then I'll look rude." Harriet fluttered her long lashes at Zach.

I bit my tongue to stop from saying something mean. "I bet it'll impress everyone here if you can fly a drone. Don't you think, Zach?"

Zach's eyes widened slightly, but then he nodded. "It could be fun to watch."

Harriet let out a dramatic sigh. "You'd be impressed by watching me fly some silly toy?"

"Sure, why not?" Zach raised his eyebrows at me.

"Let's go do it now," I said. "You'll have to open the event soon and won't want to miss your moment in the spotlight."

Harriet caught hold of Zach's elbow. "Lead the way then, handsome. I can show you how talented I am." There was more eyelash fluttering.

Zach looked at me again, and I nodded at him. I repressed every jealous feeling I had. If Harriet would reveal herself as Greg's killer, then I'd let her paw Zach for a few more minutes. But I wasn't happy about it.

Helen walked alongside me with Gunner. "Are you okay with that?" She gestured to Harriet, who had a firm grip on Zach's arm.

"Of course not! I want to tear her head off. But she thinks she can impress him by flying a drone."

"If that was Gunner, I'd be scratching her eyes out."

"I always knew you cared, princess." Gunner wrapped an arm around Helen's shoulders and pulled her toward him.

"I haven't always cared," Helen said tartly. "When we first met, I thought you were obnoxious."

"Flattery will get you everywhere." He kissed her cheek, and she giggled.

As we arrived at the drone demonstration site, several boys were already playing on the drones, supervised by an older guy wearing a baseball cap and fleecy jacket.

"Can the guest of honor have a go on a drone?" I asked him.

"Who's that?"

"That would be me." Harriet strutted forward and thrust a hand out. "Give me a controller."

The man in the cap smirked. "Of course, your Highness. I was just letting my boys have a go before the crowd gets in." He set a small black drone on the ground. "Have you ever flown one of these before?"

"How hard can it be?" Harriet said. "You hit the lever and off it goes."

"It's a little more complicated than that. The left lever moves you up and down, and the right one moves you side to side."

"I know all of this," Harriet said. She smiled flirtatiously at Zach. "I'm a fast learner. I can pick up any skill quickly."

My jealousy threatened to boil over. I clenched my hands into fists and gritted my teeth. Just another couple of minutes, and Harriet would have proved she could pilot the drone that killed Greg. My original theory would be proved right.

"Remember, the left lever takes you up and down, and the right moves you from left to right," the man said. "Have you got that?"

"I'm not an idiot," Harriet snapped. "Get out of my way." She shooed away the boys piloting the drones.

I held my breath as Harriet fiddled with the controller.

The drone wobbled on its base before shooting into the air.

"Go steady," the man in charge cautioned. "You don't want to damage it."

"I won't damage it," Harriet said. "I know what I'm doing."

"It doesn't look like it," he muttered.

The drone bounced back onto the grass and juddered along unsteadily for a few yards.

"Use the left lever to give you some height," the man said.

"That's what I'm doing." Harriet pushed the right lever from side to side.

I could see she was doing it wrong.

"Give me that!" Camilla appeared next to Harriet and grabbed the controller. "You need a gentle touch. You go jabbing the levers like that, and it'll break."

"That's what I was trying to tell her," the man in charge said. "She hasn't got a clue what she's doing, and wasn't listening to my instructions."

"I have got a clue!" Harriet stamped her foot. "It's that stupid drone. It's broken."

"It would have been if you'd kept messing around with it," the man said. "Watch what an expert can do."

Harriet folded her arms over her chest before stamping away and standing next to Zach. "I almost got it. That wasn't my fault."

"We can't be good at everything," Zach said cautiously, taking a step away from her.

Harriet shot him an evil glare.

I was focused on Camilla, who had already zoomed the drone expertly into the air and was spinning it around our heads. She banked it upward before spinning it back to the ground and then out toward the aerodrome.

"I knew you'd show us how it should be done," the man in charge said. "I used to watch you when you practiced with the drones a few months ago."

Camilla shot him a sharp look. "These things are toys. You should try piloting an RAF fighter jet."

"I'll leave that to you. You're great with these drones, though. You're even better than me, and I practice every weekend."

Camilla lowered the drone to the ground and handed him the controller. "That's enough fun for one day." Her cheeks flushed, and she glanced at me.

She must have realized she'd given herself away. She knew exactly how to pilot a drone.

"I must see to my plane," Camilla said. She raced away before I could think of an excuse to stop her.

"Ladies and gentlemen, may I have your attention please." It was the event organizer on the tannoy system. "I'm pleased to announce we are about to officially open the event. Would our honored guest, Harriet Fawcett, join me for the official ribbon cutting ceremony?"

"That's me!" Harriet grinned at Zach. "Don't go anywhere, handsome. We've got lots more fun to have today."

Zach opened his mouth, but Harriet was already hurrying away through the crowd toward her special duties. He caught hold of me and pulled me toward him. "What's going on? I know you told me to keep an eye on her, but she was getting too close for comfort."

"I'm glad to hear it," I said. "I'm letting her maul you for a good reason. At least, it was a good reason ten minutes ago." I looked over my shoulder to see if I could spot Camilla. "Now, I'm not so sure."

"Did you see how good Camilla was with that drone?" Helen hurried over with Gunner. "Even I'm doubting Harriet and Piers's involvement after that demonstration."

"What's going on?" Gunner asked. "You're having doubts? I thought you had it all figured out, and we were gathering the final bit of proof."

"It's not Harriet and Piers," I said gloomily. "They didn't kill Greg."

"What's changed your mind?" Zach asked.

"Camilla got all shifty when I asked about Greg, and she admitted she knows how to fly a drone. She just showed us how good she is."

"Alex's mom killed Greg?" Zach's eyebrows shot up. "Why would she do that?"

"I don't know, but we need to find out." I was pushed forward by the crowd gathering around the official opening ceremony. We had no choice but to follow along with them.

Harriet stood next to the mayor, a smug smile on her face as she looked at the crowd in front of her. She looked like some pompous member of the aristocracy surveying her hard working, put upon minions.

"Welcome to the tenth Old Tubbington show," the organizer said. "I'm delighted to have you all here today. As you can see, there are plenty of things to do. We're offering free flights with esteemed local resident, Camilla Hudson, a former RAF pilot and one of the first women ever to fly an RAF fighter jet. I'm sure she'll be popular all day, so make sure you sign up for your free flight. There's also the funfair if you like your rides a little more sedate."

The crowd laughed politely.

"For those who fancy flying something a little smaller than a jet, we have a drone demonstration, where you can get your hands on the controls and pilot your own drone. And we have—"

Harriet grabbed the microphone. "Yes, that's all very interesting. As the air show's honored guest, I'd like you all to have as much fun as possible. Everyone is welcome here, so long as you behave yourself." She laughed too loudly, and the microphone squealed. "And to find out what I'm up to in my fabulous, hectic social life, you can follow me on Instagram at—"

The organizer tried to take the microphone back, but Harriet scowled at him and held on tight.

He leaned close, so he could speak. "Thank you, Harriet. It's time to cut the ribbon."

I suddenly spotted Camilla. She was heading toward the aerodrome, and she had someone with her. It looked like Alex.

I shoved my way through the crowd. I needed to speak with Camilla and figure out why she'd killed Greg.

Zach joined me. "What's wrong?"

"I'm worried Camilla is going to make a run for it. She must realize she's revealed herself. We need to stop her." I headed toward the aerodrome, Zach by my side, Flipper and Jessie right behind us.

"How are you going to stop her?" he asked.

"I don't know, but we can't let her get away," I said. "I still don't know why she did it, but she must have killed Greg." I slowed as we reached the aerodrome. I could hear voices inside. It was Camilla and Alex.

"I don't understand." Alex sounded alarmed. "Why do we need to leave?"

"We both need a break," Camilla said. "You go grab a bag from the house, and we can be away from here in half an hour."

"I don't need a break," Alex said. "I need to focus on the game."

"The game can wait," Camilla said.

"No, it can't."

"Bring your research with you if you must. It's time we got out of here."

"I still don't get it," Alex said. "Why the hurry? And why do we have to fly? You know I don't like planes."

"Alex, for goodness sake. You will do this. We're leaving. Now." Camilla sounded desperate.

"Why don't you go alone?" Alex said. "You do seem tense. Take a break somewhere sunny. I can look after the house."

"No! We might be away for some time."

"Why would we do that?"

"Because we need to go!" Camilla's tone turned sharp. "Stop arguing with me and just do this."

I risked a glance into the aerodrome. Camilla held Alex by the arm.

"You're not making any sense," Alex said. "We don't need to go anywhere. We're fine here, aren't we?"

"We will be," Camilla said, "after we've had a break and gotten everything sorted."

"What do we need to sort out?" Alex was silent for a few seconds. "Is this is about the dating app?"

"I don't know what you mean," Camilla said.

"You do. I always thought it was odd the way you came to me with that app."

"Alex, stop talking nonsense. We need to go."

"No, something's wrong," Alex said. "What aren't you telling me?"

"You said you hadn't looked at that app," Camilla said. "How can you know anything is wrong?"

"I ran through the coding weeks ago. There's no way you created that."

"As I told you at the time, a friend of a friend sold me the information."

"What friend?"

"That's not important."

"It is. They must have known what they were offering you," Alex said.

"They were paid fairly."

"How much? If this goes live, it'll be worth tens of millions."

"We've discussed this already. I don't have time to go over the information again."

"Mom! I'm not going anywhere until you tell me what happened."

"You're acting as if you don't believe me." Camilla sounded hurt. "Why would I lie to you?"

"How did you get that data?"

"I... I, it's not important."

"It is." I stepped around the door. "I think your mom got it by killing Greg."

Chapter 21

Alex's face paled as he stared at me. "What are you talking about?"

Camilla scowled. "Don't listen to Lorna. She hasn't got a clue what she's talking about."

"I do," I said. "When I saw you flying that drone, I knew it had to be you."

"What do you mean?" Alex said. "Why do you think Mom killed Greg?"

"That was the thing I couldn't work out," I said, "until now. Your mom gave you the idea for a new dating app a while back?"

Alex glanced at his mom. "She did. She presented me with everything I needed. I was stunned. It was almost ready to go live."

"Alex, stop talking." Camilla caught hold of his arm again.

He pulled away from her. "I knew something was wrong. I couldn't believe all the information you had. The new app blows mine out of the water."

"The app isn't perfect," Camilla said.

"It won't need much work, though" Alex said. "When I read the coding, it looked so familiar. That's when I began to wonder about what really happened to Greg."

He looked at me. "Lorna, do you really think Mom killed Greg?"

No wonder the poor guy was so depressed. He knew something was wrong but didn't want to face up to the possibility that his mom had killed his best friend.

"That's not important," Camilla said. "Less talking and more action. We need to leave."

"It is important if you got the coding from Greg," I said. I felt Zach's reassuring presence behind me and moved closer. "You killed Greg, didn't you? You stole his business model and gave it to Alex. You killed him to stop him from telling Alex what you'd done."

Camilla looked from Alex to me.

"Mom, tell the truth," Alex said.

She let out a sigh. "I did it for your own good."

Alex moved away from Camilla. "What did you do?"

"Greg was planning on starting his own business. He was going to cut you out. I couldn't let that happen, not after how successful your original dating app had been. I couldn't allow Greg to ruin everything you'd worked so hard on."

Alex staggered back as if he'd been punched. "Greg would never do that."

"That's exactly what he was doing," Camilla said. "I overheard him talking on the phone about a new business model. I heard him say he needed to keep it from you. I knew then that he was going behind your back, selling you out, abandoning you."

Alex shook his head and raked his hands through his hair. "You've got it all wrong. Greg would never do that. We used to work on separate projects all the time. He'd go away and work out the kinks and come back to me and we'd finalize things. That was how we used to do it."

"Don't be so naïve," Camilla said. "Once I knew what he was up to, I followed him."

"You tailed my best friend?"

"He wasn't your best friend," Camilla said. "He was going to leave you out of an enormous amount of money."

"Even if he was, we already have plenty of money," Alex said. "And I'm working on the sequel to Bog Globs. Lorna's been playing it with me, and—"

"When I saw how much money this new dating app had the potential to make, I knew you had to be involved. I couldn't take the risk that Greg would sell you out."

"So you did something about it?" I asked. "You got rid of Greg and took his designs."

"I stole nothing from Greg," Camilla lifted her chin and glared at me. "You can't prove that."

It suddenly all made sense. The reason Harriet and Piers were hanging around. They were waiting for a handout from Camilla for playing their part in this. "You got Piers and Harriet to steal the information and give it to you."

Camilla glowered at me. "Where's your evidence?"

"Mom, what are you saying?" Alex asked. "You really did this?"

"I'm saying that I needed to protect my only son," Camilla said.

"By killing my best friend?"

"You have to make sacrifices when you're in combat," Camilla said. "Greg was a threat to you. He needed to be neutralized."

"He wasn't a threat. We weren't at war," Alex said. "He was my best friend. I trusted him. You've got this wrong."

The sound of running footsteps had me turning. Helen and Gunner appeared in the aerodrome.

"Is everything okay?" Helen asked. "We lost you in the crowd."

"Everything will be fine." I looked back at Camilla. "Camilla has some explaining to do to the police."

Gunner stepped forward. "Has she confessed?"

Camilla's eyes narrowed. "Who are you?"

"The police," Gunner said.

The sound of a high-pitched scream ricocheted out of the tannoy system.

I spun around and saw the crowd part. Two pigs raced away from the stage. It was Lucy and Priscilla. I stood on my tiptoes and looked at the stage. Harriet was sprawled on her back, her cream dress rumpled around her thighs and her high heels off her feet. It looked like Lucy and Priscilla had been having revenge of their own.

I noticed Piers skulking away from the side of the stage. So much for standing by your woman when she needed you.

"Mom! Wait!" Alex yelled.

I turned back and saw Camilla sprinting across the aerodrome.

Before I could move, Gunner was chasing her. He reached her in three large bounds and wrapped an arm around her. "You're not going anywhere. I've got some questions to ask you."

Camilla kicked out at Gunner, her foot connecting with his shinbone. She turned toward him and shoved him hard in the chest, knocking him off balance. She must have learned more than how to fly a jet when she was in the RAF.

"Don't fight!" Alex shouted.

Camilla looked at Alex, a sorrowful expression on her face. "I'm sorry. I thought I was doing the right thing." Then she was off again, heading toward the back door of the aerodrome.

"We can't let her get away." I chased after Camilla, but she had a good head start. I'd never catch her.

The sound of excited snorts reached me. Lucy and Priscilla shot out from under a plane and slammed straight into Camilla's legs.

She let out a startled yelp and tumbled to the ground. Both pigs rolled over, back onto their trotters, and were off again, oblivious that they had just stopped a killer.

I reached Camilla's side, gasping for breath. "Camilla Hudson, you're under arrest."

I sank onto the couch in the lounge. It felt like the end of a very long day. Gunner had arrested Camilla. She'd been taken in for questioning at the local police station. Alex had gone with her to give his side of the story.

Harriet had fled the air show, humiliated after being knocked over by the now famous pigs, Lucy and Priscilla, who were asleep in their beds after a congratulatory meal.

Piers had vanished. He was probably wondering which tropical island to escape to before the police caught up with him and asked him about stealing from Greg.

Eva was in her usual place, hidden in her bedroom, playing on her computer.

I looked at the computer screen in the lounge and sighed. Now that Alex had a resolution about what happened to Greg, I hoped he wouldn't need to spend so much time hidden from the real world. He could get out and start living.

Greg hovered by the couch, looking as lost as always.

"I thought you might be happy, now you know what happened," I said to him.

When we'd gotten back to the house, Greg had been waiting. I'd installed Zach and Gunner in the kitchen with Helen and the dogs, while she made them a late lunch, and then went to talk to him.

Greg nodded and forced a smile.

"Alex is innocent," I said. "He had nothing to do with your death. It was all a horrible misunderstanding." Sadly, a misunderstanding that had cost Greg his life.

Greg looked at the computer screen.

"Can you play computer games where you are?"

He nodded and then looked at the empty seat where Alex usually sat.

"It's not the same without Alex?"

Another nod.

"You both need to find new friends," I said. "At least, you can rest easy now, knowing your killer has been caught and Alex is innocent. He'll be okay. You both will."

Greg gave me a final nod, mouthed the words *thank you*, and then blinked out of sight.

The gloomy atmosphere lifted. Greg had gone. He wasn't happy, but he now knew what had happened to him. I hoped he got comfort from that.

"You solved the murder?" The robotic voice spoke from the speakers. It was Mickey Kill.

"It was Camilla," I said. "She killed Greg after stealing a new dating app from him with the help of Piers and Harriet. She thought Greg had gone behind Alex's back and was going to sell him out."

"He'd never do that."

"Alex knew that. So did Greg," I said. "Sadly, Camilla didn't. She said she was trying to protect Alex."

"You did a good job, Lorna Shadow."

I nodded but wondered if I would have an actual job after all of this had quietened down. Alex hadn't wanted me here. Now Camilla was gone, he might get rid of me.

"Who are you talking to?" Zach stood in the lounge doorway.

I looked at the screen. "Just a friend." I stood and walked over to him.

"Is your ghost happy?"

"Not really, but he's gone. He knows what happened. That's the best I can offer him."

"What about our ghost?" Zach took hold of my hand. "She's a problem, isn't she?"

I took a deep breath. "She is. Amelia needs to go."

"I'll do anything I can to make that happen."

I twisted my mouth to the side. I'd been thinking about our options. Zach would hate what I was about to say. "I have an idea. It might be a way to make Amelia disappear."

"I've been thinking about that too."

"What's your idea?"

"We should get married."

My jaw dropped. "How is that going to help us get rid of Amelia?"

"She'll see how serious we are about each other and leave us alone," Zach said. "Maybe that's why she's hanging around. Amelia has gotten confused and thinks we're still together."

"A ring on my finger will change her mind?"

"It might." Zach's brow furrowed. "What was your idea?"

I chewed on my bottom lip. "I was thinking I should move out."

"Move out of our home?" Zach shook his head. "No way! You can't let a ghost chase you out."

"I'm not," I said. "Until we figure out why she's there, I'm not comfortable living in the house."

"Then we'll sell," Zach said. "We'll move anywhere else. I don't care where we live, so long as we're together."

That was sweet of him. "No, that's not what I want either. I want our house back as it was before your ghostly wife visited."

"I want that too," Zach said. "I don't want you to leave. It won't solve anything."

"It will for me," I said. "I won't move far. I'll get a local job, and we can see each other every day. But until Amelia is out of the house, I'm not living in it."

"Then I'll move out with you," Zach said. "We can let Gunner and Helen have the house."

"What's this?" Helen strolled along the hallway with Gunner by her side.

"Lorna wants to leave," Zach said.

"No! I don't want to leave, but I think it's a good idea. I need distance from the Amelia problem. I need to figure out how to get rid of her. Living alongside a ghost who won't show me her problems and how I can help is frustrating."

"You're going to leave me and Gunner in a haunted house," Helen said. "Thanks for nothing."

I shook my head at her. "This isn't about you. Amelia doesn't bother you."

"She used to steal my stuff."

"At least she's not trying to steal your boyfriend," I said.

Helen huffed. "I'd like to see her try."

"What are you going to do?" Gunner asked.

"Take a break from the house," I said.

"And take a break from me?" Zach asked.

"Not for a second." I loved Zach, and I loved our home, but I needed a time out. Time to clear my head and figure out what I would do about Amelia.

"So, that's a no to marriage, as well?" Zach asked.

Helen squeaked. "Oh my goodness! Has Zach asked you to marry him?"

I looked up at Zach. "Not really."

"I will," Zach said. "The next time I do it, I'll ask properly. I'm going to make you the happiest woman on this planet."

I smiled at him. "I will be, once we get rid of Amelia and figure out what she wants. Any plans for marriage need to be put on hold until then."

Helen bounced on her toes. "I'm confused. Did Zach ask you to marry him or not?"

"No," I said.

"Yes," Zach said. "But I was being an idiot. I thought it would help."

"When we do get married, it needs to be for the right reasons, not to solve a ghostly problem."

He nodded. "You're right. One day, I will marry you."

Helen sighed. "And, one day, I'll get to design your wedding dress."

"It's a day I look forward to," I said.

Zach looked down at me. "We're okay though, aren't we?"

I hugged him. We weren't, not really. But I would make it right. I just needed to figure out how. "We'll be fine."

"Come on," Helen said, looking a bit confused by the whole are-they-aren't-they getting married discussion.

"I've just taken a tray of chocolate brownies out of the oven."

"Yum. I knew there was a reason I dated you." Gunner kissed her cheek.

She smacked his arm. "It's not just my brownies you love."

He chuckled. "Maybe not. Let's discuss it over a warm brownie and ice cream."

Zach tucked an arm around my waist. "Everything will be back to normal soon. I'm not letting you go anywhere, Lorna Shadow."

I leaned against him as we headed to the kitchen to enjoy our brownies. "You won't be able to get rid of me that easily. I can never go long without one of Helen's cakes."

He laughed and kissed me. "Same here."

As I entered the kitchen and watched my closest friends banter as they settled around the table with tea and brownies, I knew everything would turn out just fine.

***

Want to find out what's next for Lorna and Flipper?

Get **Ghostly Proposal** and meet the new ghosts in Lorna's life.

Read on to learn more.

A mysterious car crash. A house full of ghost animals. A medium with a large problem!

Lorna Shadow has had enough! When her home becomes haunted by a very unwelcome ghost, she panics and takes a local job working with a medium. Figuring that any ghost would be more interested in the medium than her, Lorna's hoping for a peaceful time, organizing paperwork as she puzzles through what to do about her own annoying ghostly problem.

Sadly, her peace lasts about ten minutes before an angry ghost appears and accuses Lorna's new boss of murder! Not only that, but the house is full of ghost animals.

Lorna needs a sit down, a cup of tea, and a slice of cake before taking on this challenge. Without Helen by her side, and things with Zach strained, Lorna feels alone and out of her depth. Still, she refuses to ignore a ghost in need of help and investigates.

Standing in her way are sneaky family members, an undertaker with a gloomy side, and a perky trainee medium who could be hiding something deadly. When a second killing takes place, Lorna realizes time is running out before the killer strikes again.

And when they do, they could be looking in her direction. Lorna's life is at risk, a ghost needs justice, and the truth must be uncovered before it's too late.

You can get **Ghostly Proposal** in e-book and paperback.

Complete series list

Ghostly Manners
Ghostly Secrets
Ghostly Games
Ghostly Affairs
Ghostly Business
Ghostly Rules
Ghostly Waves
Ghostly Play
Ghostly Proposal
Ghostly Vows
Ghostly Fright
Ghostly Hunt
Ghostly Surprises

About the Author

K.E. O'Connor (Karen) is the author of the adorably fun Lorna Shadow cozy ghost mystery series, the wickedly funny Crypt Witch paranormal mystery series, the Magical Misfits Mysteries featuring a sassy cat with a bundle of twisty puzzles to solve, the slightly darker Witch Haven paranormal mystery series featuring four troubled witches and their wonderful furry (feathered and web-slinging companions), and the whimsical, delicious Holly Holmes cozy culinary mysteries.

Stay in touch with the fun mysteries:

Newsletter: www.subscribepage.com/cozymysteries
Website: www.keoconnor.com
Facebook: www.facebook.com/keoconnorauthor